Richard Laymon was born in Chicago in 1947. He grew up in California and has a BA in English Literature from Williamette University, Oregon, and an MA from Loyola University, Los Angeles. He has worked as a school-teacher, a librarian and as a report writer for a law firm. He now works full time as a writer. Apart from his novels, he has published more than sixty short stories in magazines such as *Ellery Queen, Alfred Hitchcock* and *Cavalier* and in anthologies, including *Modern Masters of Horror, The Second Black Lizard Anthology of Crime* and *Night Visions 7.* His novel *Flesh* ws named Best Horror novel of 1988 by *Science Fiction Chronicle* and also listed for the prestigious Bram Stoker Award, as was *Funland.* Richard Laymon is the author of more than twenty acclaimed novels, including *The Cellar, The Stake, Savage, Quake, Island, Body Rides, Bite* and *Fiends.* He lives in California with his wife and daughter.

For Richard Laymon fan club information, readers may contact Martin White c/o The Ramoy Business Centre, 4 Broomfields Street, Paisley PA1 2LR. E-mail: Ramoybc@aol.com, fax: 0141 848 6669. For up-to-date cyberspace news of Richard Laymon and his books, contact Richard Laymon Kills! at: http://www.crafti.com.au/~gerlach/rlaymon.htm

# The Cellar

## Richard Laymon

First published in Great Britain in 1980
by New English Library

Published in 1989
by Star Books

Reprinted in this edition in 1991
by HEADLINE BOOK PUBLISHING

A HEADLINE FEATURE paperback

20  19  18  17  16  15  14  13

ISBN  0  7472 3533 3

Printed and bound in Great Britain by
Mackays of Chatham plc, Chatham, Kent

HEADLINE BOOK PUBLISHING
A division of Hodder Headline PLC
338 Euston Road
London NW1 3BH

To
Clayton Matthews

# The Cellar

# Prologue

Jenson grabbed the radio mike. His thumb froze on the speak button. He looked again at the upstairs window of the old, Victorian house across the street, and saw only the sheen of the moon on the glass pane. He lowered the mike to his lap.

Then a beam of light again flashed inside the dark house.

He raised the mike to his mouth. He forced his thumb down on the button. 'Jenson to headquarters.'

'Headquarters, go ahead.'

'We've got a prowler in Beast House.'

'Ten-nine, Dan. What's the matter with you? Speak up.'

'I said we've got a prowler in Beast House!'

'Jeezus! You'd better go in.'

'Send me a back-up.'

'Sweeny's ten-seven.'

'So *phone* him, for Christsake! He never eats anyplace but the Welcome Inn. Phone him.'

'Just go in, Jenson.'

'I'm not going inside that fucking place alone. You get Sweeny out here, or we can forget the whole thing.'

'I'll try to raise Sweeny. You stay put, and keep an eye on the place if you're too yellow to go in. And watch your language on the airways, buddy.'

'Ten-four.'

Patrolman Dan Jenson put down his radio mike and looked at the distant upstairs window. He saw no sign of the flashlight. His eyes moved to other windows, to the hooded darkness of the balcony over the porch, to the windows of the room with the peaked roof, then back again.

There, in the nearest window, the slim white beam of a flashlight made a quick curlicue and vanished. Jenson felt his skin shrivel as if spiders were scurrying up his back. He rolled up his window. With his elbow, he punched down the lock button of his door. The spiders didn't go away.

Inside the house, the boy was trying hard not to cry as his father pulled him by the arm from one dark room to the next.

'See? Nothing here. Do you see anything?'

'No,' the boy whimpered.

'No ghost, no boogie man, no monster?'

'No.'

'All right.'

'Can we go?' the boy asked.

'Not yet, young man. We haven't seen the attic yet.'

'She said it's locked.'

'We'll get in.'

'No. Please.'

'The monster might be waiting for us in the attic, right? Now where *was* that?' He pulled open a hall door and shined his flashlight inside. The beam illuminated an empty closet. Roughly, he pulled the boy behind him towards a door farther up the narrow corridor.

10

'Dad, let's go home.'

'Afraid the beast will get you?' The father laughed bitterly. 'We're not stepping outside this cruddy old house until you admit there *is* no beast. I won't have a son of mine cowering and whimpering his way through life, jumping at shadows, afraid of the dark.'

'There *is* a beast,' the boy insisted.

'Show it to me.'

'The guide, she said . . .'

'The guide handed us a load of bull. That's her job. You've gotta learn to know bull when it smacks you in the face, young man. Monsters are bull. Ghosts and goblins and witches are bull. And so is the beast.' He grabbed a knob, jerked open the door, and swung the beam of his flashlight inside. The staircase was a steep, narrow tunnel leading upward to a closed door.

'Come on.'

'No. Please, Dad.'

'Don't *no* me.'

The boy tried to free his arm from his father's grip, but couldn't. He began to cry.

'Stop blubbering, you little chicken.'

'I want to go home.'

The man shook him violently. 'We-are-going-up-those-stairs. The sooner we get into the attic and look for this monster of yours, the sooner we'll leave here. But not a minute earlier, do you hear me?'

'Yes,' the boy managed.

'Okay. Let's go.'

At his father's side, he started up the stairs. The wooden steps groaned and squeaked. The flashlight made a bright, small disc on each stair as they climbed. A halo surrounded the disc, dimly lighting their legs and the walls, and the next few stairs.

'Dad!'

'Quiet.'

The disc of light swung up the stairway and made a spot on the attic door high above them.

The boy wanted to sniff, but was afraid to make a sound. He let the warm fluid roll down to his upper lip, then licked it away. It tasted salty.

'See,' the father whispered. 'We're almost . . .'

From above them came a sound like a sniffing dog.

The man's hand flinched, squeezing pain into his son's arm. The boy took a single step backward, probing for the stair behind him as the attic door swung slowly open.

The flashlight beam pushed through empty darkness beyond the door.

A throaty laugh crept through the silence. It sounded to the boy like the laughter of a very old, dry man.

But it wasn't an old man who leapt through the doorway. As the flashlight dropped, its beam lit a snouted, hairless face.

When the scream came, Dan Jenson knew he couldn't wait for Sweeny. Pulling his 12-gauge Browning off its mount, he threw open the patrol-car door and leapt to the street. He dashed across it. The ticket booth was lighted by a streetlamp. The big wooden sign above it spelled 'BEAST HOUSE' in dripping letters meant to resemble blood.

He shoved the turnstile. It held fast, so he vaulted it.

More screams came from the house, screams of pain torn from a child.

Sprinting up the walkway, Jenson took the porch steps two at a time. He tried the door. Locked. He pumped a cartridge into the shotgun chamber, aimed at the lock face, and pulled the trigger. The 00 shot slammed a hole through the door. He kicked. The door whipped back. He stepped into the foyer.

From above came tearing sounds and breathless animal grunts.

Enough moonlight poured through the front windows to show him the foot of the staircase. Grabbing the bannister post, he swung himself on to the stairs. Blackness swallowed him. With one hand on the railing to guide him, he climbed. At the top of the stairs, he stopped and listened. Grunting, snarling sounds came from the left.

Cocking the shotgun, he jumped into the hallway and whirled to the right, ready to fire.

All was dark except for a puddle of brightness spilling across the hall floor. It came from the end of a flashlight.

Jenson wanted that flashlight. Needed it. But it lay far down the hall, close to the black centre of the quick, loud, gasping sounds.

Shotgun pointed up the hallway, he dashed towards the flashlight, his shoes pounding echoes, his own sharp breaths masking the rasp of the other breathing. Then his foot came down on something round like a club, but soft. Maybe an arm. His other foot kicked a hard object, and he heard its teeth clash shut as he stumbled headlong into the darkness. The shotgun mashed his fingers against the floor.

Stretching his right arm, he reached the flashlight. He swung its beam in the direction of the grunts.

The creature loosed its teeth from the nape of the boy's neck. It turned its head. The skin of its face was white and puffy like the belly of a dead fish. It seemed to smile. It writhed, freeing itself from the boy.

Jenson dropped the flashlight and tried to raise the shotgun.

He heard soft, dry laughter, and the beast took him.

# Chapter One

## 1.

Donna Hayes put down the telephone. She rubbed her trembling, wet hands on the covers, and sat up.

She had known it would happen. She had expected it, planned for it, dreaded it. Now it was upon her. 'I'm sorry to disturb you at this hour,' he'd said, 'but I knew you'd want to be informed immediately. Your husband was released. Yesterday morning. I just found out, myself. . . .'

For a long time, she stared into the darkness of her bedroom, unwilling to swing her feet down to the floor. Darkness began to fade from the room. She could wait no longer.

The Sunday morning air was like cold water drenching her skin as she stood up. Shivering, she bundled herself into a robe. She stepped across the hallway. From the slow breathing inside the room, she knew that her twelve-year-old daughter still slept.

She went to the edge of the bed. A small shoulder, covered with yellow flannel, protruded from the top of the covers. Donna cupped it in her hand and gently shook it. Rolling on to her back, the girl opened her eyes. Donna kissed her forehead. 'Good morning,' she said.

The girl smiled. She brushed pale hair away from her eyes and stretched. 'I was having a dream.'

'Was it a good one?'

The girl nodded seriously. 'I had a horse that was white all over, and so big I had to stand on a kitchen chair to get on him.'

'That sounds awfully big.'

'It was a giant,' she said. 'How come you're up so early?'

'I thought you and I might just pack our bags, get in the Maverick, and take ourselves a vacation.'

'A vacation?'

'Yep.'

'When?'

'Right now.'

'Wow!'

It took nearly an hour to wash up, dress, and pack enough clothes for a week away from the apartment. As they carried their luggage down to the carport, Donna fought a strong urge to confide in Sandy, to let the girl know that she would never return, never spend another night in her room or another lazy afternoon at Sorrento Beach, never see her school friends again. With a sense of guilt, Donna kept quiet about it.

Santa Monica was grey with its usual June morning overcast as Donna backed on to the road. She looked up and down the block. No sign of him. The prison authorities had left him at the San Rafael bus depot yesterday morning at eight. Plenty of time for him to arrive, look up her address, and come for her. But she saw no sign of him.

'Which way do you want to go?' she asked.

'I don't care.'

'How about north?'

'What's north?' Sandy asked.

'It's a direction – like south, east, west. . . .'

'Mom!'

'Well, there's San Francisco. We can see if they've painted the bridge right. There's also Portland, Seattle, Juneau, Anchorage, the North Pole.'

'Can we get there in a week?'

'We can take longer, if we want.'

'What about your job?'

'Somebody else can do it while we're gone.'

'Okay. Let's go north.'

The Santa Monica Freeway was nearly deserted. So was the San Diego. The old Maverick did fine, cruising just over sixty. 'Keep an eye out for Smokey,' Donna said.

Sandy nodded. 'Ten-four, Big Mama.'

'Watch that "Big" stuff.'

Far below them, the San Fernando Valley was sunny. The smog's yellow vapour, at this hour, was still a barely noticeable smudge hanging low over the land.

'What can your handle be?' asked Sandy.

'How about "Mom"?'

'That's no fun.'

They nosed down towards the valley, and Donna steered on to the Ventura Freeway. After a while, Sandy asked permission to change the radio station. She turned it to 93 KHJ and listened for an hour before Donna asked for an intermission, and turned the radio off.

The highway generally followed the coast to Santa Barbara, then cut inland through a wooded pass with a tunnel.

'I'm sure starving,' Sandy said.

'Okay, we'll stop pretty soon.'

They stopped at Denny's near Santa Maria. They both ordered sausage and eggs. Donna sighed with pleasure as she took her day's first drink of coffee. Sandy, with a glass of orange juice, mimicked her.

17

'That bad?' Donna asked.

'How about "Coffee Mama"?' Sandy suggested.

'Make it "Java Mama," and we've got a deal.'

'Okay, you're "Java Mama."'

'Who are you?'

'You have to name me.'

'How about "Sweetie-Pie"?'

'*Mom!*' Sandy looked disgusted.

Knowing they would have to stop for gas within an hour's driving, Donna allowed herself three cups of the dark hot coffee with breakfast.

When Sandy's plate was clean, Donna asked if she was ready to leave.

'I have to make a pit stop,' the girl said.

'Where'd you pick *that* up?'

Sandy shrugged, grinning.

'Uncle Bob, I bet.'

'Maybe.'

'Well, I have to make a pit stop, too.'

Then they were on the road again. Just north of San Luis Obispo, they pulled into a Chevron station, gassed up the Ford, and used the toilets. Two hours later, in the bright heat of the San Joaquin Valley, they stopped at a drive-in for Cokes and cheeseburgers. The valley seemed to go on forever, but finally the freeway curved upward to the west, and the air lost some of its heat. The radio began to pick up San Francisco stations.

'Are we almost there?' Sandy asked.

'Where?'

'San Francisco.'

'Almost. Another hour or so.'

'That long?'

'Afraid so.'

'Will we spend the night?'

'I don't think so. I want to go tar, don't you?'

'How far?' Sandy asked.

'The North Pole.'

'Oh, *Mom*.'

18

It was after three o'clock when Highway 101 sloped downward into a shadowy corner of San Francisco. They waited at a stoplight, turned, watched for signs marking 101, and turned again: up Van Ness Avenue, left on to Lombard, finally up a curving road to the Golden Gate.

'Remember how disappointed you were the first time you saw it?' Donna asked.

'I'm still disappointed. If it isn't golden, they shouldn't say it is. Should they?'

'Certainly not. It is beautiful, though.'

'But it's orange. Not golden. They ought to call it the Orange Gate.'

Glancing out towards the open sea, Donna saw the front edge of a fog mass. It looked pure white in the sunlight. 'Look at the fog,' she said. 'Isn't it lovely?'

'It's okay.'

They left the Golden Gate behind.

They passed through a tunnel with a mouth painted like a rainbow.

They sped by the Sausalito off-ramp.

'Hey, can we go to Stinson Beach?' Sandy asked, reading the sign for the turn-off.

Donna shrugged. 'Why not? It won't be as fast, but it'll be a lot prettier.' She flicked on her turn signal, followed the curving ramp, and left 101 behind.

Soon they were on the Coast Highway. It was narrow: far too narrow and far too crooked, considering the steep drop just across the left-hand lanes. She drove as far to the right as the road would allow.

The fog lay just offshore, as white and heavy as cotton batting. It seemed to be moving slowly closer, but was still a good distance away from shore when they reached the town of Stinson Beach.

'Can we spend the night here?' Sandy asked.

'Let's keep going for a while. Okay?'

'Do we have to?'

'You've never been to Bodega Bay?'

'No.'

'That's where they filmed that movie *The Birds*.'

'Oooh, that was scary.'

'Should we try for Bodega?'

'How far is it?' the girl asked.

'Maybe an hour.' She ached, especially in her back. It was important, though, to keep going, to put more miles behind them. She could stand the pain for a while longer.

When they reached Bodega Bay, Donna said, 'Let's keep going for a little while.'

'Do we have to? I'm tired.'

'*You're* tired. *I'm* dying.'

Soon after they left Bodega Bay, fog started to blow past the windshield. Fingers of it began reaching over the lip of the road, sneaking forward, feeling blindly. Then, as if they liked what they felt, the whole body of fog shambled on to the road.

'Mom, I can't see!'

Through the thick white mass, Donna could barely make out the front of the hood. The road was only a memory. She stepped on the brakes, praying that another car hadn't come up behind them. She steered to the right. Her wheels crunched gravel. Suddenly the car plunged down.

2.

An instant before the stop threw Donna into the steering wheel, she flung an arm across her daughter's chest. Sandy folded at the hips, knocking the arm away. Her head hit the dashboard. She started to cry. Donna quickly turned off the engine.

'Let's see.'

The soft dashboard had left a red mark across the girl's forehead.

'Are you hurt any place else?'

'Here.'

20

'Where the seat belt got you?'

She nodded, gulping.

'Good thing you had it on.' Her mind pictured Sandy's head breaking through the windshield, jagged glass ripping her body, then the last of her disappearing into the fog, forever lost.'

'Wish I hadn't.'

'Let's undo it. Hold on.'

The girl braced herself against the dash, and Donna unlatched the seat belt.

'Okay, let's get out now. I'll go first. Don't do anything until I say it's all right.'

'Okay.'

Climbing out, Donna slipped on the fog-wet grassy covering of the slope. She clung to the door until she found her footing.

'Are you okay?' Sandy asked.

'So far, so good.' Holding herself steady, she peered through the fog. Apparently the road had curved to the left without them, and they had nose-dived into a ditch. The rear of the car remained at road level: unless the fog was too thick, it would be visible to passing cars.

Donna worked her way carefully down the slippery embankment. The Maverick's front bumper was buried in the ditch. Steam hissed from the crevices of the hood. She crawled across the hood, got down on the other side, and climbed the slope to Sandy's door. She helped the girl out. Together they slid and stumbled to the bottom of the ditch.

'Well,' Donna said, in a voice as cheerful as she could muster, 'here we are. Now let's have a look at your wounds.'

Sandy untucked her plaid blouse and lifted it out of the way. Donna, squatting, lowered the girl's jeans. A wide band of red crossed her belly. The skin over her hip bones looked tender and raw, as if layers had been sandpapered off. 'I'll bet that stings.'

Sandy nodded. Donna began to lift the jeans.

'I've gotta go.'

'Well, pick a tree. Just a second.' She climbed up to the car and took a box of Kleenex from the glove compartment. 'You can use these.'

Carrying the box of tissue with one hand and holding up her jeans with the other, Sandy walked along the bottom of the ditch. She vanished in the fog. 'Hey, here's a path!' she called.

'Don't go far.'

'Just a little ways.'

Donna heard her daughter's feet crushing the forest mat of dead twigs and pine needles. The sounds became faint. 'Sandy! Don't go any farther.'

The footfalls had either stopped, or faded so completely with distance that they blended with the other forest sounds.

'Sandy!'

'What?' The girl sounded annoyed, but her voice came from far away.

'Can you get back all right?'

'Geez, Mom.'

'Okay.' Donna leaned back until the seat of her corduroy pants pressed against the car. She shivered. Her blouse was too thin to keep out the cold. She would wait for Sandy, then get jackets out of the back seat. Until the girl's return, she didn't want to move. She waited, staring into the grey where Sandy had gone.

Suddenly, the wind tore away a shred of fog. 'That was a longer-than average pit stop,' Donna said.

Sandy didn't answer, or move.

'What's the matter, hon?'

She just stood there, above the ditch, motionless and mute.

'Sandy, what's wrong?'

Feeling a prickling chill on the back of her neck, Donna snapped her head around. Nothing behind her. She looked back at Sandy.

'My God, what's wrong?'

Pushing from the car, she ran. She ran towards the paralysed, silent figure at the forest edge. Ran through the grey, obscuring murk. Watched the shape of her daughter twist into a crude resemblance as the fog thinned until, a dozen feet away, nothing remained of Sandy but a four-foot pine sapling.

'Oh, Jesus,' Donna muttered. And then she shrieked, 'Sandy!'

'Mom,' came the distant voice. 'I think I'm lost.'

'Don't move.'

'I won't.'

'Don't move. Stay right where you are! I'm coming!'

'Hurry!'

A narrow path through the pines seemed to point in the voice's direction. Donna hurried.

'Sandy!' she shouted.

'Here.'

The voice was closer. Donna walked quickly, watching the fog, stepping over a dead pine trunk blocking the path.

'Sandy?'

'Mom!'

The voice was very close now, but off to the right.

'Okay, I've almost reached you.'

'Hurry.'

'Just a minute.' She stepped off the path, pushing between damp limbs that tried to hold her back. 'Where are you, darling?'

'Here.'

'Where?'

'Here!'

'Where?' Before the girl could answer, Donna shoved through a barrier of branches and saw her.

'Mom!'

She was clutching the pink box of Kleenex to her chest as if it would somehow keep her from harm.

'I got turned around,' she explained.

Donna hugged her. 'That's all right, honey. It's all right. Did you take care of business?'

She nodded.

'Okay, let's go back to the car.'

If we can find it, she thought.

But she found the path without difficulty, and the path took them to the opening above the ditch. Donna kept her eyes down as she stepped past the pine sapling she had mistaken for Sandy. Silly, she knew, but the thought of seeing it frightened her; what if it looked like Sandy again, or like someone else – a stranger, or *him?*

'Don't be mad,' Sandy said.

'Me? I'm not mad.'

'You look mad.'

'Do I?' She smiled. Then the two of them climbed down the slope of the ditch. 'I was just thinking,' Donna said.

'About Dad?'

She forced herself not to react. She didn't gasp, didn't suddenly squeeze her daughter's hand, didn't let her head snap towards the girl in shock. In a voice that sounded very calm, she said, 'Why would I be thinking about Dad?'

The girl shrugged.

'Come on. Out with it.'

Ahead of them, the dark bulk of the car appeared through the fog.

'I was just thinking about him,' Sandy told her.

'Why?'

'It was scary back there.'

'Is that the only reason?'

'It was cold, like that time. And I had my pants down.'

'Oh God.'

'I got afraid he might be watching.'

'I bet that was plenty scary.'

'Yeah.'

They stopped at the side of the car. Sandy looked up

at Donna. In a very small voice Sandy said, 'What if he gets us here? All by ourselves?'

'Impossible.'

'He'd kill us, wouldn't he?'

'No, of course not. Besides, it can't happen.'

'It might, if he escaped. Or if they let him out.'

'Even if they did, he'd never find us here.'

'Oh yes he would. He told me so. He said he'd find us wherever we went. He said, "I'll sniff you down."'

'Shhhh.'

'What?' Sandy whispered.

For a moment, Donna held to the hope that it was only the sound of the ocean surf beating the rocky shore. But the surf was across the road, and far down the cliff. Besides, why hadn't she heard it before now? The sound grew.

'A car's coming,' she muttered.

The girl's face went pale. 'It's *him!*'

'No, it's not. Get in the car.'

'It's him. He escaped! It's him!'

'No! Get in the car. Quick!'

### 3.

She first saw the man in the rear-view mirror, hunched over the back of the car, turning his head slowly as he looked in at her. His tiny eyes, his nose, his grinning mouth, all seemed far too small, as if they belonged to a head half the size of this one.

A gloved fist knocked on the rear window.

'Mom!'

She looked down at her daughter crouched on the floor below the dashboard. 'It's okay, honey.'

'Who is it?'

'I don't know.'

'Is it *him?*'

'No.'

The car rocked as the stranger's hand tugged the door handle. He knocked on the window. Donna turned to him. He looked about forty, in spite of the deep lines carved in his face. He seemed less interested in Donna, than in the plastic head of the lock button. He pointed a gloved finger at it, pecking the window glass.

Donna shook her head.

'I'll come in,' he called.

Donna shook her head. 'No!'

The man smiled as if it were a game. 'I'll come in.' He let go of the door handle and leapt to the bottom of the ditch. When he hit the ground, he almost fell. Steadying himself, he glanced over his shoulder as if to see whether Donna had appreciated his jump. He grinned. Then he started hobbling along the ditch, limping badly. The fog nibbled at him. Then he was gone.

'What's he doing now?' Sandy asked from the floor.

'I don't know.'

'Did he go away?'

'He's in the ditch. I can't see him. The fog's too thick.'

'Maybe he'll get lost.'

'Maybe.'

'Who is he?'

'I don't know, honey.'

'Does he want to hurt us?'

Donna didn't answer. She saw a dark shape in the fog. It slowly became distinct, became the strange, limping man. In his left hand he carried a rock.

'Is he back?' Sandy asked.

'He's on his way.'

'What's he doing?'

'Honey, I want you to sit up.'

'What?'

'Get up in your seat. If I tell you to, I want you to jump out and run. Run into the woods and hide.'

'What about you?'

'I'll try to come, too. But you go when I say, regardless.'

26

'No. I won't go without you.'

'Sandra!'

'I won't!'

Donna watched the man climb up the embankment to the car. He used the door handle to pull himself up. Then he thumped the window, like before, pointing at the lock button. He made a smile. 'I'll come in,' he said.

'Go away!'

He raised the grey, wedge-shaped rock in his left hand. He tapped it lightly against the window, then looked at her.

'Okay,' Donna said to him.

'Mom, don't.'

'We can't stay in here,' she said quietly.

The man grinned as Donna reached over her shoulder.

'Get ready, hon.'

'No!'

She flicked up the lock button, levered the door handle and thrust herself against it. The door swung, jolted, and knocked into the man. With a yelp of surprise, he tumbled backward, the rock flying from his hand. He did a crooked somersault to the bottom of the ditch.

'Now!'

'Mom!'

'Let's go!'

'He'll get us!'

Donna saw him motionless on his back. His eyes were shut. 'It's all right,' she said. 'Look. He's knocked out.'

'He's playing possum, Mom. He'll get us.'

Hanging on to the open door, one foot down on the slippery grass, Donna stared at the man. He certainly *looked* unconscious, the way his arms and legs were splayed out in such strange, grotesque ways. Unconscious, or even dead.

Playing possum?

She raised her foot inside the car, pulled the door shut, and locked it. 'Okay,' she said, 'we'll stay.'

The girl sighed, and lowered herself, once again, to the floor in front of the seat.

Donna managed a smile for her. 'You okay?'

She nodded.

'Cold?'

Another nod. Awkwardly, Donna turned and stretched an arm over the back of the seat. She reached Sandy's coat first, then her own.

Curled against the passenger door, Sandy used the coat to cover all but her face.

Donna got into her blue windbreaker.

The man outside hadn't moved.

'It's almost dark,' Sandy whispered.

'Yeah.'

'He'll come for us when it's dark.'

'Do you have to say that kind of stuff?'

'I'm sorry,' the girl said.

'Besides, I don't think he's coming for anybody. I think he's hurt.'

'He's pretending.'

'I don't know.' Bent forward with her chin on the steering wheel, Donna watched him. She watched for the movement of an arm or leg, for a turn of the head, an opening eye. Then she tried to see if he was breathing.

In his fall, the sweatshirt under his open jacket had pulled up, leaving his belly exposed. She watched it closely. It didn't seem to be moving, but the distance was enough that she could easily miss the subtle rise and fall of his breathing.

Especially under all that hair.

He must be a mass of hair from head to toe. No, the head was shaved. Even the top. There seemed to be a bristly crown of dark stubble on top, as if he hadn't shaved it for several days.

He ought to shave his belly, she thought.

She looked at it again. Still, she couldn't see any movement.

His grey pants hung low on his hips, showing the

waistband of his underwear. Baggy boxer shorts.
Striped. Donna looked down at his feet. His sneakers
were soiled grey, and held together with tape.

'Sandy?'

'Hmmm?'

'Stay inside.'

'What are you doing?' Fright in the girl's voice.

'I'm going out for a second.'

'No!'

'He can't hurt us, honey.'

'Please.'

'I think he might be dead.'

She opened the car door and climbed out carefully.
She locked the door. Shut it. Tried it. Fingering the side
of the car for balance, she eased herself down the slope.
She stood above the man. He didn't move. She zipped
her windbreaker, and knelt beside him.

'Hey,' she said. She jiggled his shoulder. 'Hey, are
you okay?'

She pressed a hand flat against his chest, felt its rise
and fall, felt the light throbbing of his heart.

'Can you wake up?' she asked. 'I want to help you.
Are you hurt?'

In the growing darkness, she didn't notice the moving,
gloved hand until it grabbed her wrist.


4.


With a startled yelp, Donna tried to twist free. She
couldn't break the man's stiff grip.

His eyes opened.

'Let go. Please.'

'It hurts,' he said.

His hand squeezed more tightly. His grip felt strange.
Glancing down, Donna saw that he was holding her with
only two fingers and the thumb of his right hand. The

other two glove fingers remained straight. With a vague stir of revulsion, she realized there were probably no fingers inside those parts of the glove.

'I'm sorry it hurts,' Donna said, 'but you're hurting me, now.'

'You'll run.'

'No. I promise.'

His tight grip eased. 'I wasn't going to hurt you,' he said. He sounded as if he might cry. 'I just wanted in. You didn't have to hurt me.'

'I was frightened.'

'I just wanted in.'

'Where are you hurt?'

'Here.' He pointed at the back of his head.

'I can't see.'

Groaning, he rolled over. Donna saw the pale shape of a rock on the ground where his head had been. Though the night was too dark to be certain, there didn't seem to be blood on his head. She touched it, feeling the soft brush of his hair stubble, and found a lump. Then she inspected her fingers. She rubbed them together. No blood.

'I'm Axel,' the man said. 'Axel Kutch.'

'I'm Donna. I don't think you're bleeding.'

'Dah-nuh.'

'Yes.'

'Donna.'

'Axel.'

He got to his hands and knees and turned his face to her. 'I just wanted in.'

'That's okay, Axel.'

'Do I have to go now?'

'No.'

'Can I stay with you?'

'Maybe we can all go away. Will you drive us somewhere for help?'

'I drive good.'

Donna helped him to stand. 'Why don't we wait for the fog to lift, then you can drive us somewhere for help.'

'Home.'

'Your home?'

He nodded. 'It's safe.'

'Where do you live?'

'Malcasa Point.'

'Is that nearby?'

'We'll go there.'

'Where is it, Axel?'

He pointed into the darkness. North.

'We'll go home. It's safe.'

'Okay. But we have to wait for the fog to lift. You wait in your car, and we'll wait in ours.'

'Come with me.'

'When the fog lifts. Good-bye.' She feared he would try to stop her from getting into the car, but he didn't. She shut the door and rolled down the window. 'Axel?' He limped closer. 'This is my daughter, Sandy.'

'San-dee,' he said.

'This is Axel Kutch.'

'Hi,' Sandy greeted him, her voice soft and uncertain.

'We'll see you later,' Donna said. She waved goodbye and rolled up the window.

For a few moments, Axel stared silently in at them. Then he climbed the slope and was gone.

'What's wrong with him?' the girl asked.

'I think he's . . . slow.'

'You mean a retard?'

'That's not a nice way to put it, Sandy.'

'We've got them like that at school. Retards. Know what they're called? Special.'

'That sounds a lot better.'

'Yeah, I guess. Where'd he go?'

'Back to his car.'

'Is he leaving?' Sandy's voice was eager with hope.

'Nope. We'll wait for the fog to thin out, then he's going to drive us out of here.'

'We're going in his car?'

'Ours isn't going any place.'

31

'I know, but . . .'

'Would you rather stay here?'

'He scares me.'

'That's just because he's strange. If he wanted to do us harm, he's had plenty of opportunity. He certainly couldn't find a better location for it than right here.'

'Maybe, maybe not.'

'Anyway, we can't just stay here.'

'I know. Dad'll get us.' The girl's eyes were black holes in the oval of her face. 'Dad's not in prison anymore, is he?'

'No, he's not. The district attorney . . . remember Mr Goldstein? . . . he telephoned this morning. They let Dad out yesterday. Mr Goldstein called to warn us.'

'Are we running away?'

'Yes.'

The girl on the floor lapsed into silence. Donna, resting against the steering wheel, closed her eyes. At some point, she fell asleep. She was awakened by a quiet sob.

'Sandy, what is it?'

'It won't do any good.'

'What won't?'

'He'll get us.'

'Honey!'

'He *will!*'

'Try to sleep, honey. It'll be all right. You'll see.'

The girl became silent except for an occasional sniff. Donna, leaning on the steering wheel, waited for sleep. When it finally came, it was a tense, aching half-sleep feverish with vivid dreams. She stood it as long as she could. At last, she had to get out. If the rest of her body could endure the torment, her full bladder couldn't.

Taking the box of Kleenex from the floor beside Sandy, she climbed silently from the car. The chilly air made her shake. She breathed deeply. Rolling her head, she tried to work the stiffness out of her sore neck muscles. It didn't seem to help much. She locked the door and pushed it quietly shut.

Before letting go of its handle, she looked over the top of the car. On the shoulder of the road, less than twenty feet from the rear of the Maverick, was a pick-up truck.

Axel Kutch sat on the roof of its cab, legs hanging over the windshield. His face, turned skyward, was lighted by a full moon. He seemed to be staring at it, as if entranced.

Silently, Donna crept down the slope. From the bottom of the ditch, she could still see Axel's head. She watched it as she opened her corduroys. The huge head was still tilted back, its mouth gaping. She crouched close to the car.

The breeze was cold on her skin.

*I was cold, like that time. And I had my pants down.*

Everything will be fine, she thought.

*He'll sniff us down.*

When she finished, Donna climbed the slope to the roadside. Axel, sitting on the roof of his truck cab, didn't seem to notice.

'Axel?'

His hands flinched. He looked down at her and smiled. 'Donna,' he said.

'The fog's gone. Maybe we can leave now.'

Without a word, he jumped down. When he hit the asphalt road, his left leg buckled, but he kept his balance.

'What's going on?' Sandy called to them.

'We're leaving.'

The three of them unpacked the Maverick and transferred the suitcases to the bed of the pick-up truck. Then they climbed inside, Donna sitting between Axel and her daughter.

'Help me remember where the car is,' she told Sandy.

'Will we come back for it?'

'We sure will.'

Axel steered his truck on to the road. He grinned at Donna. She grinned back.

'You smell good,' he said.

She thanked him.

Then he was quiet. On the radio, Jeannie C. Riley sang about the Harper Valley PTA. Donna fell asleep before the end of the song. She opened her eyes, sometime later, saw the truck's headlights opening a path through the darkness of the curving road, and shut them again. Later, she was awakened when Axel started to sing along in his thick, low voice, with 'The Blind Man in the Bleachers.' She drifted again into sleep. A hand on her thigh woke her up.

Axel's hand.

'Here we are,' he said. Lifting the hand away, he pointed.

The headlights lit a metal sign: 'WELCOME TO MALCASA POINT, pop. 400. Drive with Care.'

Looking ahead through the bars of a wrought-iron fence, Donna saw a dark, Victorian house: a strange mixture of bay windows, gables, and balconies. At one end of the roof, a cone-shaped peak jabbed at the night. 'What's this place?' she asked in a whisper.

'Beast House,' said Axel.

'*The* Beast House?'

He nodded.

'Where the murders were?'

'They were fools.'

'Who?'

'They went in at night.'

He slowed the truck.

'What are you . . . ?'

He turned left on to an unpaved road directly across from the ticket booth of Beast House. Ahead of them, perhaps fifty yards up the road, stood a two-story brick house with a garage.

'Here we are,' Axel said.

'What *is* this?'

'Home. It's safe.'

'Mom?' Sandy's voice was like a moan of despair.

34

Donna took the girl's hand. The palm was sweaty.

'It's safe,' Axel repeated.

'It doesn't have windows. Not a single window.'

'No. It's safe.'

'We're not going in there, Axel.'

## 5.

'Isn't there some place else we can spend the night?' Donna asked.

'No.'

'Isn't there?'

'I want you here.'

'We won't stay here. Not in *that* house.'

'Mother's here.'

'It's not that. Just take us some place else. There has to be some kind of motel or something.'

'You're mad at me,' he said.

'No, I'm not. Just take us some place else, where we can stay till morning.'

He backed the pick-up on to the road, and drove through the few blocks of Malcasa Point's business section. At the north end of town was a Chevron station. Closed. Half a mile beyond it, Axel pulled into the lighted parking lot of the Welcome Inn. Overhead, a red neon sign flashed the word 'VACANCY.'

'This is just fine,' Donna said. 'Let's just unload our luggage, and we'll be all set.'

They climbed from the truck. Reaching into the back, Axel pulled out the suitcases.

'I'll go home,' he said.

'Thanks a lot for helping us like you did.'

He grinned and shrugged.

'Yeah,' said Sandy. 'Same here.'

'Wait.' His grin became very big. Reaching into a hip pocket, he pulled out his billfold. The black leather looked old, shiny with a dull gloss from so much use, and ragged at the corners. It flopped open. He spread the lips of its bill compartment, which was bloated more with a thick assortment of papers and cards than with money. Holding the billfold inches from his nose, he searched it. He began to mutter. He looked at Donna with a silent plea for patience, then made a quick, embarrassed smile at Sandy. 'Wait,' he said. Turning his back to them, he ducked his head and bit the fingertps of his right-hand glove.

Donna glanced at the motel office. It looked empty, but lighted. The coffee shop across the driveway was crowded. She could smell french fries. Her stomach rumbled.

'Ah!' Glove hanging from his teeth, Axel swung around. In his hand – or what there was of a hand – he held two blue cards. The skin of his hand was seamed with scars. Half-inch stumps remained of the two missing fingers. The tip of his middle finger was gone. Two flesh-coloured bandages wrapped his thumb.

Donna took the card, smiling in spite of the heavy thickness she suddenly felt in her stomach. She started to read the top one. 'COMPLIMENTARY' was printed in block letters. The small type beneath it was difficult to see in the lights of the parking lot, but she struggled with it, reading aloud. 'This ticket entitles the bearer to one free, guided tour of Malcasa Point's infamous, world-renowned Beast House. . . .'

'Is that the scary old place with the fence?' Sandy asked.

Axel nodded, grinning. Donna saw that his glove was on again.

'Hey, that'd be neat!'

'I work there,' he said, looking proud.

'Is there really a beast?' the girl asked.

'Just at night. No tours after four.'

'Well, thank you for the tickets, Axel. And for driving us here.'

'Will you come?'

36

'We'll try to see it,' Donna said, though she had no intention of touring such a place.

'Are you the tour guide?' asked Sandy.

'I clean. Scrub-a-dub-dub.' Waving at them, he climbed into his truck. Donna and Sandy watched it roll out of the parking lot. It disappeared down the road towards Malcasa Point.

'Well.' Donna took a deep breath, relishing the relief she felt at Axel's departure. 'Let's get registered, and then we'll grab a bite to eat.'

'A bite won't be enough.'

'We'll buy the joint out.'

They picked up their suitcases and walked towards the motel office.

'Can we take the tour tomorrow?' Sandy asked.

'We'll see.'

'Does that mean no?'

'If you want to go on the tour, we'll do it.'

'All right!'

# Chapter Two

Roy rang the doorbell of Apartment 10 and waited. He heard nothing from inside. He jammed the button five times, quickly.

Goddamn bitch, why wouldn't she open up?

Maybe she's not home.

She has to be home. Nobody's out on a Sunday night, not at eleven-thirty.

Maybe she's asleep.

He pounded the door with his knuckles. Waited. Pounded again.

Down the hallway, a door opened. A man in pyjamas looked out. 'Knock it off, would you?'

'Go fuck yourself.'

'Look, buddy . . .'

'You want me to kick the shit out of you, just say one more word.'

'Get out of here, or I'll call the cops.'

Roy started towards him. The man slammed the door. Roy heard the rattle of a guard chain.

Okay, the guy's probably dialling right now.

It'd take the cops a few minutes to get here. He decided to use those minutes.

Bracing himself against the wall opposite Apartment 10, he threw himself forward. The heel of his upraised shoe caught the door close to the knob. With a crash, the door shot open. Roy ducked, slid up his right pants leg, and unsheathed the Buck knife he'd bought that day at a sporting goods store. Knife out, he entered the dark apartment.

He turned on a lamp. Crossed the living room. Rushed down a short hallway. The bedroom on the left, probably Sandy's room, was deserted. Same with the one on the right. He opened its closets. Most of the hangers were bare.

Shit!

He ran out of the apartment, down the stairs, and out the back way to the alley. Across the alley was a row of garages. He ran past the end garage and found a gate. He pushed it open. A walkway led down the side of an apartment building. He followed it to the street.

No cars coming.

He dashed across.

This block had houses instead of apartment buildings. Much better. He crouched behind a tree and waited for a car to pass. When it was gone, he started along the sidewalk, inspecting each house, looking for the one that seemed most promising.

He chose a small, stucco house that was dark at the windows. He didn't choose it because of the darkness, he chose it because of the girl's-style bicycle he saw in the front yard.

Careless, leaving it there.

It could've been stolen. Maybe they thought the little fence would protect it.

The fence wouldn't protect anything.

40

Roy reached over the gate and carefully lifted the latch. The gate squeaked as he pushed it open. He shut it gently and hurried up the walkway to the front stoop. The door had no peephole. That would make things easier.

He knocked hard and fast. He waited a few seconds, then hit the door three more times.

Light appeared in the living-room window.

'Who's there?' a man asked.

'Police.' Roy backed away and crouched slightly, right shoulder towards the door.

'What do you want?'

'We're evacuating the neighbourhood.'

'What?'

'We're evacuating the area. A gas main broke.'

The door opened.

Roy lunged. The guard chain snapped taut. It's mounting shot from the doorjamb. The door slammed into the man, knocking him backward. Roy dived into him, covered his mouth, and jabbed the knife into his throat.

'Marv?' a woman called. 'What's going on out there?'

Roy shut the front door.

'Marv?' Fear in her voice. 'Marv, are you all right?'

Roy heard the whirr of a spinning telephone dial. He ran to the hall. Near the end, light shone through an open door. He rushed towards it. He was almost there when a girl stepped out of a dark doorway, glanced at him, and gasped. Roy grabbed her hair.

'Mommy!' Roy called. 'Hang up the phone or I cut your daughter's throat.'

'God in heaven!'

'Let me hear it.' He yanked the girl's hair. She cried out.

The phone clattered. 'It's down! I put it down!'

Roy twisted the girl's hair, making her turn around. 'Walk,' he said. Knife blade poised across her throat, he walked behind her to the far bedroom.

41

The woman stood next to her bed, stiff and trembling. She wore a white nightgown. Her pale arms were crossed tightly as if she were trying to warm herself.

'What . . . what did you do to Marv?'

'He's all right.'

Her eyes lowered to Roy's knife hand. He glanced down. His hand was shiny red. 'So I lied,' he said.

'God in heaven! O merciful God!'

'Shut up.'

'You killed him!'

'Shut up.'

'You killed my Marv!'

He shoved the girl roughly towards the bed and ran at the hysterical woman. Her mouth gaped wide to scream. Clutching the front of her nightgown, he jerked her forward and punched the knife into her stomach. She sucked air as if her wind had been knocked out. 'Gonna shut up now?' Roy asked, and stabbed again.

She started to sag, so Roy let go of the nightgown. She sank to her knees, both hands pressing her belly. Then she slumped forward.

The girl on the bed didn't move. She just stared.

'Now, you don't want to get stabbed, too, do you?' he asked her.

She shook her head. She was trembling. She looked ready to scream.

Roy glanced down at himself. His shirt and pants dripped blood. 'I guess I'm a mess, aren't I?'

She said nothing.

'What's your name?'

'Joni.'

'How old are you, Joni?'

'I'll be ten.'

'Why don't you come along and help me clean up?'

'I don't want to.'

'Do you want me to stab you?'

She shook her head. Her lips trembled.

'Then come with me.' Taking her hand, he pulled her

42

off the bed. He led her down the hallway until he found the bathroom. He turned on its light, and pulled her inside.

The bathroom was long, with a sink and counter close to the door, a space, and then the toilet. The bathtub, set into the wall opposite the toilet, had frosted shower doors.

Roy led the girl to the toilet. The seat was already down. Its green, fuzzy cover matched the carpet. 'Sit there.'

Joni obeyed.

Kneeling in front of her, Roy unfastened the buttons of her pyjama top. She sobbed. 'Knock that off.' He slipped the pyjamas down her arms. 'We'll get good and clean,' he said. He unsnapped the waistband, tugged the pants out from under her, and down her legs. She clamped her knees together. Arms crossed over breasts no more developed than a boy's, she bent far down, bringing her shoulders almost to her knees.

Roy turned on the hot water. As it splashed into the tub, he undressed himself. When all his clothes lay heaped on the floor, he plugged the bathtub drain. He adjusted the water so it was hot, but not scalding.

Joni still sat on the toilet seat, hunched over and hugging her knees.

Roy grabbed her arm. She tried to pull free, so he slapped the side of her head. She yelped, but didn't move. Standing in front of her, Roy grabbed both arms and jerked her to her feet. She cried, 'No!' as he swung her into the bathtub. Her feet whipped. She kicked the metal spout and cried out in pain. Roy nearly lost his grip but managed to keep from falling backward. She splashed the water, rump first. Roy climbed in, facing her.

He knelt in the water. 'I've about had it,' he warned. 'Sit still.'

She kicked. Her heel caught him in the thigh.

'Okay.'

43

Clutching her ankles, he lifted her legs and pulled her forward. Her head slipped underwater. Her eyes and mouth were puckered shut. Her hands slapped the sides of the tub, reached up blindly for something to hold, found nothing, and splashed water. Roy watched the frantic girl, enjoying the struggle, excited by the sight of her skinny body and the cleft at the hairless joining of her legs.

He let her ankles down. The girl's face broke the surface, eyes and mouth gaping as if surprised. She gasped air. Roy let her sit up.

'No more trouble,' he said.

She sniffed, and wiped her runny nose with the back of her hand. Then she crossed her arms and bent forward.

Roy twisted sideways. He turned off the cold faucet, and let just the hot water run for a while. The water level rose. Soon it was good and hot and deep. He turned off the water.

'Let's switch places,' he said. Standing, he stepped over her. She scooted forward, her rump squeaking on the enamel. Roy sat down, leaned against the cool back of the tub, and stretched out his legs on each side of her.

'Now we'll get all clean,' he said.

He lifted a bar of soap from its tray and began to rub her back. When that was slick, he eased her closer so she was reclining against him. Reaching over her shoulders, he soaped her chest, her belly. Her skin was warm, pliant, slippery. He pulled her more tightly against him. He put the soap in the tray. He reached down between her legs.

That's when the mother staggered up to the tub, raising a butcher's knife. Roy's left hand rammed the sliding door shut. The knife point thumped the door, and scraped down it. Roy shoved the girl forward. He kneed her away. Pressing the edge of the door to keep it shut, he got his feet under him. The mother lurched sideways. Her left hand let go of her sopping, bloody

44

nightgown and reached for the rear half of the sliding door. Roy held it shut with his other hand. As if there were no door, the women plunged the knife towards Roy's face. It's point hit, shaking the door. She stabbed again and again. The sound from her throat was part growl, part an outcry of pain or frustration.

Joni gripped Roy's leg and started to pull.

'Bitch! Let go!'

He released the right-hand door long enough to bat Joni's face with the back of his fist. Her head jerked with the impact. It thudded the tile wall.

The mother reached for the free door. Roy got to it first and held it shut. Growling with rage, she grabbed the top runner of the doors. She climbed and pulled herself until she was standing on the tub's edge. Her face appeared above Roy, eyes wild. She swung her right arm down, slashing towards him. He ducked below the knife's arc.

Inches from his eyes, the mother's red, clinging nightgown smeared blood on the door. She was pressed tightly to the door, her bare feet on the rim of the tub.

She grunted. The blade *whished* above him. She propped her left knee on the towel bar halfway up the door.

Shit, she's climbing it!

Roy jerked the door. It slid open, slamming the wall at the front of the tub. Reaching forward with both hands, he clutched the woman's right ankle. He pulled. His hands slipped on the bloody skin, but he kept his grip. With a cry of horror, she flopped backward. She hit the floor first with the back of her head. She went limp. Still holding her right ankle, Roy climbed out of the tub. He picked up her other leg and swivelled her away from the tub.

He picked up her knife. He cut her throat with it, then returned to the tub.

Joni, sitting sideways, looked up at Roy with blank eyes.

He squatted in the tub. The water felt tepid. He turned on the hot water. When the temperature felt hot enough, he turned the water off and stepped to the rear of the tub.

He sat and leaned back.

Taking Joni under the arms, he slid her close between his spread legs until he could feel the press of her against his penis.

'Now,' he said, and picked up the soap. His throat was tight. This was what he'd wanted for so long, so long. This was what he'd always wanted. 'Now,' he said, 'we're all set.'

# *Chapter Three*

### 1.

The Nubian guards, dressed like pimps, came at Rucker from all sides. Their black faces were glossy with sweat, their big teeth white and shiny. Some aimed handguns at his face, other began spraying him with automatic fire from AK-47 assault rifles. He cut them down, but more came running, shrieking, brandishing cutlasses. His American 180 stitched holes across their bright shirts. They fell, but more came.

Where the hell are they coming from? he wondered.

From Hell.

He kept firing. One hundred and seventy rounds in six seconds. A mighty long six seconds.

They still came. Some had spears. Some, now, were naked.

He dropped the ammo drum, stuffed another into place, and kept firing.

Now all of them were naked, their black skin shimmering in the moonlight, their smiles big and white. None had guns. Only knives, swords, and spears.

I've killed all the pimps, he thought. Who're these? The reserves. When I get them, I'll be home free.

But stark fear whispered a message of death in his ear. Looking down, he saw the alloy barrel of his rifle droop, melting.

Oh Jesus, oh Jesus, they're gonna get me now. They'll lay me low. They'll cut off my head. Oh Jesus!

Gasping, heart racing, he bolted upright. He was alone in the bedroom. A trickle of sweat slid down his back. He ran a hand through his wet hair and wiped it dry on the sheet.

He looked at the alarm clock.

Only five past midnight. *Damn.* This was a lot earlier than usual. When the nightmares got him at four or five, he could go out for breakfast and start the day. When they got him this early, it was bad.

He got out of bed. The sweat on his naked body turned cold. In the bathroom, he dried himself with a towel. Then he put on a robe and went into the living room of the apartment. He turned on all the lights. Then the television. He flipped through the channels. *The Bank Dick* was on. It must've started at twelve. He got a can of Hamms from the refrigerator, a can of peanuts from the cupboard, and returned to the living room.

As he reached for the flip-tab, he watched his hand shake.

It never shook on a job.

*Judgement Rucker's got balls of brass.*

If they could only see him now.

It's those damned nightmares.

Well, those would ease off. They always did. Just a matter of time.

Watch the movie.

He tried.

When he ran out of beer, he went into the kitchen for

another. He popped its tab and looked out the window. Moonlight made a silver path on the water. Across the bay, fog matted the hills above Sausalito as white as a bank of snow. Fog wrapped most of the Golden Gate Bridge, too. All but the top of its northern tower, with its red flashing light, was hidden in fog. Probably the other tower was poking through, too, but Belvedere Island blocked that part of his view. He listened to the low groan of a foghorn, then carried his beer into the living room.

He was about to sit on the couch when a harsh, male scream of horror slashed the stillness.

## 2.

Jud listened at the door of Apartment 315. From inside came the sound of a man taking quick gasps of air. Jud rapped the door quietly.

At the end of the hallway, a woman in curlers peered out her doorway. 'Let's keep it down, huh? You can't keep it down, I'll call the cops. Do you know what time it is?'

Jud smiled at her. 'Yes,' he said.

The anger pinching her face seemed to let go. She made a tentative smile. 'You're the new tenant, aren't you? The one in 308? I'm Sally Leonard.'

'Go to bed now, Miss Leonard.'

'Something the matter with Larry?'

'I'll take care of it.'

Still smiling, Sally pulled her head back inside her apartment and shut the door.

Jud knocked again on 315.

'Who is it?' a man asked through the door.

'I heard a scream.'

'I'm sorry. Did it wake you?'

'I was already up. Who screamed?'

'Me. It was nothing. Just a nightmare.'

49

'You call that nothing?'

Jud heard the slide of a guard chain. The door was opened by a man in striped pjamas. 'You sound as if you know nightmares,' the man said. Though his sleep-tangled hair was as white as the fog, he seemed to be no older than forty. 'My name's Lawrence Maywood Usher.' He offered his hand to Jud. It was bony, and damp with sweat. The feeble grip had a weariness that seemed to sap strength from Jud's hand.

'I'm Jud Rucker,' he said, entering.

The man shut the door. 'Well, Judson . . .'

'It's Judgement.'

Larry immediately perked up. 'As in Judgement Day?'

'My father's a Baptist minister.'

'Judgement Rucker. Fascinating. Would you care for some coffee, Judgement?'

He thought about the open can of Hamms in his apartment. What the hell, he could use it tomorrow for cooking. 'Sure, Coffee'd be great.'

'Are you a connoisseur?'

'Hardly.'

'Nevertheless, this should be a treat for you. Have you ever tasted Jamaican Blue Mountain?'

'Not that I know of.'

'Well, opportunity has knocked. Your ship has come in.'

Jud grinned, astonished at the new liveliness of the man who'd screamed.

'Will you join me in the kitchen?'

'Sure.'

In the kitchen, Larry opened a small brown bag. He tilted its opening towards Jud's face. Jud sniffed the sharp coffee aroma. 'Smells good,' he said.

'It ought to be. It's the best. What line of work are you in, Judgement?'

'Engineering,' he said, using his usual cover.

'Oh?'

'I'm with Brecht Brothers.'

'Sounds like a German coughdrop.'

'We build bridges, power plants. How about you?'

'I teach.'

'High school?'

'God forbid! I had my fill of those rude, insolent, foul-mouthed bastards ten years ago. Never again! God forbid!'

'What do you teach now?'

'The elite.' He cranked, grinding down the coffee beans. 'Upper division, mostly, at USF. American Lit.'

'And they're not foul-mouthed?'

'The oaths are not directed at *me*.'

'That would make a difference,' Jud said. He watched the man spoon coffee grounds into the basket of a drip machine and turn it on.

'*All* the difference. Shall we sit down?'

They went into the living room. Larry took the sofa. Jud lowered himself into a recliner, but didn't recline.

'I'm certainly glad you dropped by, Judgement.'

'How about Jud?'

'How about Judge?'

'I'm not ever a lawyer.'

'From your looks, however, you are a good judge. Of character, of situations, of right and wrong.'

'You can tell all that from my looks?'

'Certainly. So I'll call you Judge.'

'All right.'

'Tell me, Judge, what possessed you to come knocking at my door?'

'I heard the scream.'

'Did you realize it was inspired by a nightmare?'

'No.'

'Perhaps I was being murdered.'

'That occurred to me.'

'But you came, nonetheless. And unarmed. You must be a fearless man, Judge.'

'Hardly.'

'Or perhaps you've known such fear that the possibility of being confronted by a mere murderer seemed trifling.'

Jud laughed. 'Sure.'

'Nonetheless, I'm certainly glad you came. For terrors of the night, there's no antidote like a friendly face.'

'Do you have your terrors often?'

'Every night for the past three weeks. Not quite three weeks – that would be twenty-one nights, and I've only had the nightmares for the past nineteen. Only! I must tell you, it seems like years.'

'I know.'

'Sometimes, I wonder if there ever was a time before the nightmares. Of course, there was. I'm not loony, you realize, just upset. Nervous, very very dreadfully nervous I had been and am; but why *will* you say that I am mad?'

'I didn't.'

'No, of course not.' He grinned with one side of his mouth. 'That's Poe. "The Tell-Tale Heart." About another distressed fellow. Distressed to the point of madness. Do I look mad?'

'You look tired.'

'Nineteen nights.'

'Do you know what triggered your nightmares?' Jud asked.

'Let me show you.' From beneath a *Time* magazine on the coffee table, he took a newspaper clipping. 'You may read this while I see to the coffee.' He got up from the sofa and handed the news article to Jud.

Alone in the room, Jud eased back on the recliner and read:


### THREE SLAIN IN BEAST HOUSE

(MALCASA POINT) – The mutilated bodies of two men and an eleven-year-old boy were found late Wednesday night in Malcasa Point's grisly tourist attraction, Beast House.

According to local authorities, police patrolman Daniel Jenson entered the house at 11:45 P.M. to investigate possible prowlers. When he failed to contact headquarters, a car was dispatched to the location. With the aid of the volunteer fire department, officers cordoned off the area and entered the mysterious house.

The body of Patrolman Jenson was found in the upstairs corridor, along with the bodies of Mr Matthew Ziegler and his son, Andrew. All three were the victims of apparent knife assault.

According to Mary Ziegler, wife of the deceased, Matthew was angered by their son's frightened reaction to a public tour of Beast House earlier in the day, and vowed to 'show him the beast.' Shortly after 11 P.M. Wednesday night, he drove the boy to Beast House with the intention of breaking in and forcing young Andrew to 'face up to' his fears.

Beast House, built in 1902 by the widow of Lyle Thorn, leader of the infamous Thorn Gang, has been the scene of no fewer than eleven mysterious killings since the time of its construction. The present owner, Maggie Kutch, moved out of the house in 1931 after her husband and three children were 'torn asunder by a raving white beast' that reportedly entered the house through a downstairs window. Shortly after the brutal slayings, Mrs Kutch opened the house for daylight tours.

No further incidents were reported until 1951, when two twelve-year-old boys, residents of Malcasa Point, entered the house after dark. One boy, Larry Maywood, escaped with minor injuries. The mutilated body of his friend, Tom Bagley, was found at dawn by investigators.

Commenting on the most recent slayings, the seventy-one-year-old owner of the house explained, 'After dark, it belongs to the beast.' According to Malcasa

53

Point Police Chief Billy Charles, 'No beast is responsible for the deaths of Patrolman Jenson and the Zieglers. They were slain by a man wielding a sharp instrument. We expect to apprehend the perpetrator in short order.'

Beast House tours have been suspended for an indefinite period, pending completion of the homicide investigation.

Jud sat forward in the recliner and looked at Larry's nervously smiling face as the man brought two cups of coffee into the room. He accepted one of the cups. He waited for Larry to sit down. Then he said. 'You introduced yourself as Lawrence Maywood Usher.'

'I've always been a great admirer of Poe. In fact, I suppose, it was largely his influence that inspired me to explore Beast House that night with Tommy. It seemed only fitting, when I finally decided a new name was essential for my emotional survival, to take the name of Poe's haunted Roderick Usher.'

### 3.

Lawrence Maywood Usher sipped coffee from his fragile, bone-china cup. Jud watched him hold the liquid in his mouth like wine, savouring it before swallowing. 'Ah, delicious.' He looked eagerly at Jud.

Jud lifted his cup. He liked the heavy aroma, and took a sip. It tasted stronger than he preferred. 'Not bad,' he said.

'You're a master of understatement, Judge.' Concern furrowed the gaunt man's face. 'You *do* like it?'

'It's fine. Very good. I'm just not used to this kind of thing.'

'Never become *used* to anything you love. It blunts the edge of appreciation.'

Jud nodded and took another drink. This time the

coffee tasted better. 'Are your nightmares about Beast House?' he asked.

'Always.'

'I'm surprised it took a newspaper story to start them, considering what you must've gone through at the time.'

'The story, more or less, reactivated the nightmares. I had them constantly for several months following my . . . encounter. Doctors suggested psychiatric treatment, but my parents wouldn't hear of it. Perceptive people that they were, they considered psychiatry to be the pursuit of fools and madmen. We moved away from Malcasa Point, and my nightmares rather quickly lost their intensity. I've always considered it a victory of common sense over quackery.' He smiled, apparently delighted by his wit, and indulged himself in another taste of coffee.

'Unfortunately,' he continued, 'we weren't entirely able to leave the incident behind. Every now and then, an eager journalist would track us down for a story on the miserable tourist attraction. That would always start the nightmares again. Every major magazine, of course, has done the story.'

'I've seen a couple of them.'

'Did you read them?'

'No.'

'Lurid bunk. Reporters! Do you know what a reporter is? "A writer who guesses his way to the truth and dispels it with a tempest of words." Ambrose Bierce. The single time I did allow one of those scavengers to interview me, he twisted my words so that I appeared a gibbering idiot. He concluded that the encounter had unhinged me! After that, I changed my name. Not one of those bastards has tracked me down, so far, and I've been free of nightmares about the beast until now . . . now that it's killed again.'

'It?'

'Officially, since the time of the attack on the Thorns, it's been a *he*, a knife-wielding maniac, something on the

55

order of Jack the Ripper. Each attack, of course, is a different killer.'

'And it's not?'

'Not at all. It's a beast. Always the same beast.'

Jud didn't try to conceal the expression of doubt he knew was beginning to appear on his face.

'Let me refill your cup, Judge.'

### 4.

'I don't know what the beast is,' Larry said. 'Perhaps nobody knows. I've seen it, though. With the exception of old Maggie Kutch, I'm probably the only living person who has.

'It is not human, Judge. Or if it *is* human, it's some kind of unspeakable deformity. And it is very, very old. The first known attack occurred in 1903. Teddy Roosevelt was President then. That's the year the Wright brothers flew at Kitty Hawk, for heaven's sake. The beast killed three people that year.'

'The original owner of the house?'

'She survived. That was Lyle Thorn's widow. Her sister, though, was killed. So were Lilly's two children. The authorities blamed the atrocity on a mental defective they found on the outskirts of town. He was tried, convicted, and hanged from the house balcony. Even then, apparently, cover-up was the order of the day. They *had* to know the fellow was innocent.'

'Why did they have to know that?'

'The beast has claws,' Larry said. 'They're sharp, like nails. They shred the victim, his clothes, his flesh. They pierce him to hold him down, while the beast . . . violates him.' The cup began to clatter against its saucer. He set it down on the table and folded his hands.

'Were you . . .?'

'My God, no! It never touched me. Not *me*. But I saw what it did to Tommy there in the bedroom. It was too

. . . overcome . . . to bother with me. It had to finish with Tommy, first. Well, I put one over on it! The window gave me some nasty cuts, and I broke my arm in the fall, but I got away. I got away, goddamn it! I lived to tell the tale!'

He managed another drink of coffee. His trembling hand set the cup back down on the table. The drink seemed to help restore his calm. In a quiet voice, he said, 'Of course, no one believes the tale. I've learned to keep it to myself. Now I suppose you think I'm mad.' He looked at Jud, despair in his weary eyes.

Jud pointed towards the newspaper clipping. 'That says eleven people have died in Beast House.'

'Its facts are correct, for a change.'

'That's a lot of killing.'

'Indeed.'

'Somebody should put a stop to it.'

'I'd kill it myself, if I had the courage. But God, to think of entering that house at night! Never. I could never do it.'

'Has anybody gone in after it?'

'At night? Only a fool . . .'

'Or a man with a very good reason.'

'What kind of reason?' Larry asked.

'Revenge, idealism, money. Has a reward ever been offered?'

'For killing it? Its existence isn't even *admitted*, not by anyone but old Kutch and her crazy son. And they certainly don't want it harmed. That goddamned beast, and its reputation, is their sole source of income. It's probably all that keeps the town afloat, for that matter. Beast House is no Hearst Castle or Winchester House, but you'd be surprised how many people will pay four bucks a head for a guided tour of an old place that not only boasts a legendary monster but that also was the scene of eleven brutal murders. They come from all over California, from Oregon, from every state in the union. A family driving through California can't pass within fifty miles of Malcasa Point without its kids screaming to tour Beast House. Tourist dollars are the lifeblood of the town. If somebody were to kill the beast . . .'

'Think of the tourists its carcass would bring,' Jud suggested, grinning.

'But the mystery would be gone. The beast is the heart of that house. The house would die without it. Malcasa Point would follow close on its heels, and the people don't want that.'

'They'd rather have the killing continue?'

'Certainly. An occasional killing does wonders for business.'

'If the town is that way, it doesn't deserve to live.'

'A perceptive man your father was, naming you Judgement.'

'You said you would kill the beast yourself, if you could.'

'If I had the courage, yes.'

'Have you ever thought of hiring someone to do it for you?'

'Who could I hire for a job like that?'

'Depends on what you're willing to pay.'

'What's a good night's sleep worth, eh?' The grin on his hollow face looked grotesque.

'You might look upon it as a contribution to humanity,' Jud said.

'I assume you know someone who might be willing, for a large sum of money, to enter the house at night and dispatch the beast?'

'I might know someone,' Jud told him.

'What would it cost?'

'That depends on the risk involved. He'd have to know a lot more before making a firm commitment.'

'Can you give me a rough idea?'

'His minimum would be five thousand.'

'His maximum?'

'No maximum.'

'My funds aren't bottomless, but I believe I'd be

willing to invest a considerate portion of them, if necessary, in a project of that type.'

'What are you doing tomorrow?'

'I'm open to suggestions,' Larry said.

'Why don't the two of us drive up the coast, bright and early, and pay a visit to Beast House.'

## 5.

The two cups of coffee didn't keep Jud awake when he got back to his apartment. He fell asleep at once, and if he dreamed at all, he remembered none of it when the alarm clock blared at 6 A.M. Monday.

# *Chapter Four*

Roy woke up in a king-sized bed. Next to him, face down with her hands tied behind her back, lay the girl Joni. She was naked. A short length of clothesline led from her wrists to Roy's right hand. He untied his hand, then both of hers.

He rolled Joni on to her back. Her eyes were open. She looked up at him, through him, past him. Almost as if she were blind.

'Sleep well?' he asked.

She didn't seem to hear.

He placed a hand on her chest, feeling the steady beat of her heart, and the rise and fall of her breathing.

'Where's your spirit?' he asked, and laughed.

She didn't blink or move. Not when he pinched her. Not when he stroked her body, nor sucked it, or bit it. Not when he entered her. Not when he shuddered with an orgasm. Not when he pulled out and got off the bed.

He tied her again, anyway.

He dressed in the father's clothes. He made coffee. While it percolated, he prepared six slices of bacon, three eggs over easy, and two pieces of toast. He carried them into the living room and turned on the television.

The phone rang. He picked it up.

'Hello?' he asked.

'Hello?' The woman's voice sounded confused. 'May I speak to Marv, please?'

'He isn't here. Can I take a message?'

'This is Esther. His secretary?'

'Oh. You must be wondering why he didn't show up at work.'

'He didn't even call in.'

'Oh, well, no. He had a heart attack last night. Early this morning, actually.'

'No!'

'I'm afraid so. Last I saw, they were loading him into an ambulance.'

'Is he . . . is he alive?'

'Last I heard. I'm staying with Joni. You know, baby-sitting. I haven't heard a thing since they left.'

'What hospital was he taken to, do you know?'

'Let me think. Gee, you know, I'm not really sure. Everything was so confused.'

'Could you let us know when you hear any word of his condition?'

'I'd be glad to.'

She gave him the office telephone number. He didn't copy it. 'I'll be sure to get back to you,' he said, 'the minute I get any news.'

'Thank you so much.'

'You're welcome.'

He hung up, went back to the couch, and began to eat. His breakfast was still warm.

When he finished it, he searched for the telephone book. He found it in a kitchen drawer under a wall extension. He poured himself another cup of coffee and returned to the living room.

First, he looked up Hayes. No Hayes, Donna. Only the Hayes, D., that he had checked last night. It had been her apartment, no question about that. He'd recognized some of the furniture.

He wondered if she still worked for that travel agency. What was its name? Had a catchy slogan. 'Let Gold be your guide? Not gold, Gould. Gould Travel. He thumbed through the white pages, found it, and dialled.

'Gould Travel Service, Miss Winnow.'

'I'd like to speak to Mrs Hayes, please.'

'Hayes?'

'Donna Hayes.'

'We have no Donna Hayes at this number. This is Gould Travel Service.'

'She works there, or she *did*.'

'Just a moment, please.' He waited for almost a minute. 'Sir, Donna Hayes left our employ several years ago.'

'Do you know where she went?'

'I'm afraid not. May I be of service to you? Were you thinking of a cruise, perhaps? We have some marvellous cruises. . . .'

'No thank you.' He hung up.

He looked up Blix, John. Donna's father. Her parents would know where she'd gone, for sure. He copied the address and phone number.

Shit, he didn't want to see them. They were the last people he wanted to see.

What about Karen? He grinned. He wouldn't mind seeing Karen, at all. In fact, he wouldn't mind seeing a lot of her. Maybe she'd know where to find those two bitches.

Worth a try.

Even if she didn't know, a visit could still turn out worthwhile. He'd always liked the looks of her.

What was the name of that guy she'd married? Bob something. Something like a candy bar. Milky Way? No. Mars Bar. Bob Mars Bar. Marston.

He looked up Marston, found a Robert, and copied the address and telephone number.

He'd pay them a nice visit. Not now. He didn't want to leave quite yet. What was the hurry? He might as well stick around for a while, enjoy himself.

He went into the bedroom. 'Hi there, Joni. What you been up to?'

She stared at the ceiling.

# Chapter Five

## 1.

Sunlight and screeching seagulls woke Donna. She tried to fall asleep again, but the narrow bed, sway-backed with age, made it impossible. She got up and stretched her stiff muscles.

Sandy was still asleep on the other bed.

Quietly, Donna crossed the cool wood floor to the front window. She raised the blind and looked out. Across the courtyard, a man weighted down with suitcases was leaving a small, green-painted cabin. A woman and a matching pair of children waited for him inside a station wagon. Half the cabins of the Welcome Inn had either a car or a camper parked in front. Somewhere nearby, a dog barked. She pulled the blind.

Then she looked for the telephone. The room didn't have one.

While she was dressing, Sandy woke up.

'Morning, honey. Did you sleep well?'

'Fine. Where are you going?'

'I want to find a telephone and call Aunt Karen.' She tied her sneakers. 'I don't want her worrying about us.'

'Can I come?'

'You can stay here and get dressed. I'll only be a minute, then we'll go get some breakfast.'

'Okay.'

She buttoned her plaid cotton blouse and picked up her handbag. 'Don't open the door for anyone, right?'

'Right,' the girl said.

Outside, the morning air was fresh with the scent of pine, a smell that reminded her of warm, shadowed trails in the Sierra where she used to backpack with her sister. Before Roy. The way Roy acted in the mountains, she quickly lost the taste for the wilderness. Once she was rid of him, she should have taken up backpacking again. Maybe soon . . .

She climbed steps to the porch of the motel office and saw a telephone booth at the far end. She headed for it. The wood groaned under her feet, sounding like the weathered planking of an aged pier.

She stepped into the booth, dropped coins into the telephone slot, and dialled Operator. She charged the call to her home phone. The call went through.

'Hello?'

'Morning, Karen.'

'Uh-oh.'

'Is that any kind of greeting?'

'Don't tell me, your car broke down.'

'You're clairvoyant.'

'Do you need a lift?'

'No, I'm afraid I'll have to beg off, for today.'

'Poor loser.'

'It's not that.'

'They changed your days off? And we were having such good times on Mondays. What've you got now, Friday-Saturday, Tuesday-Wednesday?'

'Your clairvoyance has slipped.'

'Oh?'

'I'm calling from the glamorous resort town of Malcasa Point, home of the infamous Beast House.'

'Are you crocked?'

'Sober, unfortunately. As near as I can figure, we're about a hundred miles north of San Francisco. Give or take fifty.'

'Christ almighty, don't you know?'

'Not exactly. I'm sure, if I could see a map . . .'

'What are you doing way the hell-and-gone up there, anyway?' Before Donna could answer, Karen said, 'Oh God, is he out?'

'He's out.'

'Oh my God.'

'We thought we'd better make ourselves scarce.'

'Right. What do you want me to do?'

'Let Mom and Dad know we're okay.'

'What about your apartment?'

'Can you have our stuff put into storage?'

'Sure, I guess.'

'Call Beacon, or someone. Let me know what it comes to, and I'll send you a cheque.'

'How am I gonna let you know anything?'

'I'll keep in touch.'

'Are you ever coming back?'

'I don't know.'

'How could they let him *out*? How *could* they?'

'I guess he behaved himself.'

'Christ!'

'It'll be all right, Karen.'

'When am I gonna *see* you again?' She sounded close to tears.

'This'll blow over.'

'Sure it will. If Roy happens to drop dead of a coronary, or drives into a bridge abutment, or . . .' A sob broke her voice. 'Christ, this sort of thing . . . how can they let it happen?'

67

'Hey, don't cry. Everything'll be fine. Just tell Mom and Dad we're okay, and we'll be in touch.'

'Okay. And I'll . . . take care of your apartment.'

'Take care of yourself, while you're at it.'

'Sure. You too. Tell Sandy hi for me.'

'I will. Goodbye, Karen.'

'Bye.'

Donna hung up. She breathed deeply, fighting for control of her own shaken emotions. Then she crossed the porch. As she started to climb down, she heard the squeak of an opening door.

'Lady?'

She looked around at a teenage girl standing in the office doorway. Probably the owner's daughter. 'Yes?'

'Are you the lady with the car trouble?'

Donna nodded.

'Bix from the Chevron called. Him and Kutch went after it. Bix said he'd see you when he gets back.'

'They don't have the keys.'

'Bix doesn't need 'em.'

'Did he want me to do anything?'

The girl shrugged one shoulder. It was bare except for the strap of her tank top. She was obviously wearing no bra, her nipples pressing dark and turgid against the thin fabric. Donna wondered why the girl's parents allowed her to dress that way.

'Okay. Thanks for the message.'

'Any time.'

The girl spun away. Her cut-off jeans were slit up the sides, revealing tawny leg almost to the hip.

The girl's going to get herself raped, Donna thought. If Sandy ever dressed like that . . .

Donna climbed down the porch steps and crossed the parking area to their cabin. She had to wait while Sandy finished in the bathroom.

'Do you want to eat here at the Inn?' Donna asked. 'Or should we try our luck in town?'

'Let's go into town,' Sandy said, her voice eager. 'I

hope they've got Dunkin' Donuts. I'm dying for a doughnut.'

'I'm dying for a cup of coffee.'

'Java Mama.'

They went outside. Sandy, squinting, opened her denim handbag and took out her sunglasses. Their round lenses were huge on her face. Donna, who rarely wore sunglasses, thought they made her daughter look like a bug – a *cute* bug, bit still a bug. She was careful never to mention the resemblance.

'What did Aunt Karen say?' Sandy asked.

'She said to tell you hi.'

'Were you gonna play tennis today?'

'Yep.'

'I bet she was surprised.'

'She understood.'

They reached the roadside. Donna pointed to the left. 'Town's that way,' she said. They started towards it. 'From the way Aunt Karen sounded, I don't think she'd ever heard of Malcasa Point. It is a beautiful place, though, isn't it?'

Sandy nodded. Her sunglasses slipped down her nose. With a forefinger, she poked them into place. 'It's pretty around here, but . . .'

'What?'

'Oh, nothing.'

'No, tell me. Come on.'

'How come you told Aunt Karen?'

'Told her what?'

'Where we are.'

'I thought she ought to know.'

'Oh.' Sandy nodded, and adjusted her glasses.

'Why?'

'Do you think it was a good idea, telling her? I mean, now she knows where we are.'

'She won't tell anyone.'

'Not unless he *makes* her.'

They stepped off the roadside and waited on the rutted shoulder until an approaching car whooshed by.

'What do you mean, "*makes* her"?' Donna asked.

'Makes her tell. Like he used to make you tell things.'

Donna walked in silence, no longer enjoying the cool, piny air. She imagined her sister stretched naked on a bed, tied firm, Roy beside her using a cigarette lighter to heat the shaft of a screwdriver.

'You never saw what he did to me, did you? He always locked the door.'

'Oh I never saw *that*. Not what he did in the bedroom. Just when he hit you. What *did* he do in the bedroom?'

'He hurt me.'

'It must've been awful.'

'Yeah.'

'How did he hurt you?'

'Lots of ways.'

'I bet he does that to Aunt Karen.'

'He wouldn't dare,' Donna said. 'He wouldn't dare.'

'When can we leave here?' the girl asked nervously.

'As soon as the car's ready.'

'When'll that be?'

'I don't know. Axel went out there this morning with a man from the service station. If it doesn't need repairs, we can go as soon as they get here with it.'

'We'd better,' Sandy said. 'We'd better get out of here fast.'


2.


They chose to eat breakfast at Sarah's Diner across from the Chevron station. After seeing the selection of dough-nuts displayed on a counter-top cake stand, Sandy decided against them. She ordered bacon and eggs, instead.

'This place is gross,' she said.

'We won't eat here from now on.'

'Ha ha.'

Sandy put a hand underneath the table, and crinkled her nose with disgust. 'There's *gum* under the table.'

'There's always gum under tables. Some of us have sense enough to keep our hands off it.'

Sandy sniffed her fingers. 'Gross.'

'Why don't you go wash your hands?'

'I bet the john is *really* the pits,' she said, and got up from the table as if eager to verify her theory.

Smiling, Donna watched her step smartly towards the far end of the diner. The waitress came and filled Donna's heavy, chipped cup with coffee.

'Thank you.'

'Welcome, sweetie.'

She watched the waitress head for another table. Then the opening door caught her eyes.

Two men entered the diner. The emaciated one seemed far too young to have white hair. Though nicely dressed in a blue leisure suit, he had a harassed look like a refugee. The man beside him might have been his keeper. With deep blue eyes in a face that made her think of carved, highly polished wood, he had the confident look of a cop. Or a soldier. Or the guide in Colorado, many years ago, who led her and Karen on a deer hunt with their father.

The two men sat at the counter. The strong one had light brown hair neatly clipped above his shirt collar. His wide back filled the tan shirt, pulling it taut. The black belt looked stiff and new in jeans so old that one of the belt loops hung loose, dangling over his rear pocket. His rubber-soled hiking boots looked older than the jeans.

As if attracted by the intensity of her gaze, the man looked over his shoulder. Donna fought an urge to turn away. She met his eyes for a moment, then glanced at the next man, then on down the counter casually. She lifted her coffee cup. Steam no longer rose from the coffee. An oily film on the dark surface reflected swirling

71

colours like a rainbow, or spoiled roast beef. She drank, anyway. Setting down the cup, she allowed herself another glance at the man.

He was no longer watching her.

Disappointment shadowed Donna's relief.

She drank more coffee and watched him. His head was turned as he listened to the nervous, white-haired man. A shoulder blocked her view of his mouth. She saw a slight rise on the ridge of his nose, apparently from an old break. A scar slanted from the corner of his eyebrow down to his cheekbone. She looked back into her coffee, afraid she might again attract attention.

When she heard quick, familiar footsteps, she saw the man's head turn. He glanced at Sandy, then Donna, then looked back at his friend.

'All clean?' Donna asked, perhaps too loudly.

'They didn't have anything to dry my hands on,' Sandy told her, and sat down.

'What'd you use?'

'My pants. Where's the food?'

'Maybe we'll be lucky and it won't come.'

'I'm starved.'

'I guess we can give it a try.'

The waitress soon came, bringing plates of eggs, sausage links, and hash browns. The food looked good, oddly enough. As Donna sliced into her sausage, her stomach rumbled loudly.

'Mother!' Sandy giggled.

'Must be a thunderstorm on the way,' Donna said.

'Can't trick me. That was your gut.'

'Gut isn't polite, honey.'

The girl grinned. Then, with an expression of wrinkled distaste, she picked a sprig of parsley off her hash browns and flicked it over the edge of the plate.

Donna glanced at the man. He was drinking coffee. As she ate and talked with Sandy, she looked up at him often. She realized that he wasn't eating. Apparently he

72

and his friend had only come into Sarah's for coffee. Soon they got up from the counter.

The man reached into his hip pocket as he headed for the cash register. His nervous friend protested, and lost. After he paid the bill, he took a thin cigar out of his shirt pocket. He unwrapped it. As he wadded its cellophane wrapper into a tiny ball, he scanned the area near the counter, probably searching for a trash container. Finding none, he stuffed the ball into his shirt pocket. He clamped the cigar between his teeth. His eyes swung suddenly towards Donna. They fixed upon her, held her stunned like a doe in headlights. The eyes stayed on her while the man struck a match and sucked its flame to the tip of his cigar. He shook out the match. Then he turned, and pushed through the door.

Donna let out a deep, trembling breath.

'You okay?' Sandy asked.

'I'm fine.'

'What's wrong?'

'Nothing. Everything's fine.'

'You don't look so fine.'

'Are you about done eating?'

'All done,' Sandy said.

'Ready to go?'

'*I* am. Aren't you gonna finish?'

'No, I don't think so. Let's be on our way.' She picked up the bill. Her hand shook as she reached into her purse. She tucked three quarters under the edge of her plate, and got up quickly.

'What's wrong?'

'I just want to get outside.'

'Okay,' the girl said doubtfully as she followed Donna to the cash register.

Outside, Donna looked down the sidewalk. A block off, an old woman with a poodle was stepping awkwardly off a curb. No sign of the two men from the cafe. She checked the other direction.

'What're you looking for?' Sandy asked.

'Just trying to decide which way looks best.'

'We've already been that way,' the girl said, and nodded towards the left.

'Okay.' So they turned right, and began walking.

'Do you think we can leave this morning?' Sandy asked.

'I don't know how long it'll be. I think we're a good hour or so from where we left the car. The girl at the motel didn't say what time Axel went to get it.'

'If we aren't gonna leave right away, can we go see Beast House?'

'I don't know, honey.'

'It's half-price for me.'

'Are you certain you really want to see a place like that?'

'What is it?'

'It's supposed to be the home of a horrible beast that kills people and tears them up. It's where those three people were murdered a few weeks ago.'

'Oooh, *that* place?'

'Yes indeed.'

'Wow! Can we see it?'

'I'm not sure I'm up to it.'

'Oh come on. We're almost there. Please?'

'Well, it wouldn't hurt to see what time the tours start.'

### 3.

Standing at the northern corner of the wrought-iron fence, Donna looked at the bleak, weathered house and felt a reluctance to approach it.

'I'm not sure I want to do this, honey.'

'You *said* we can check on the tours.'

'I'm not sure I want to go in there, at all.'

'Why not?'

Donna shrugged, unwilling to put words to her dark chill. 'I don't know,' she said.

She moved her eyes from the slanted bay window to the veranda with its balustraded balcony overhead, past a gable to a tower at the south end. The tower windows reflected emptiness. Its roof was a steep cone: a witch's cap.

'Afraid it'll gross you out?'

'Your language is enough to gross me out.'

Sandy laughed, and adjusted her slipping sunglasses.

'Okay, we'll have a look at the tour schedule. But I'm not guaranteeing anything.' They started towards the ticket booth.

'I'll go alone, if you're scared.'

'You will not go in there alone, young lady.'

'It's half-price for me.'

'That's not the point.'

'What *is*?'

*You might never come out*, Donna suddenly thought. She took a deep breath. The air, scented like high mountain pine, calmed her.

'What is the point?'

Donna made her grin as evil as she could, and muttered, 'I don't want the beast to eat you.'

'You're awful!'

'Not as awful as the beast.'

'Mother!' Laughing, Sandy swung her denim handbag.

Donna blocked it with her forearm, looked up, and saw the man from the cafe. His eyes were on her. Smiling at him, Donna fought off another assault by her daughter.

She saw a blue ticket in his hand.

'Okay, honey, that's enough. We'll go on the tour.'

'Can we?' she asked, delighted.

'Shoulder to shoulder, we'll confront the awful beast.'

'I'll smash it with my purse,' Sandy said.

As she approached the line at the gate, Donna saw the man turn casually to his nervous friend and start talking.

'Look.' Sandy pointed at a wooden clockface near the top of the ticket booth. The sign above it read, 'Next tour departs at,' and the clock indicated ten. 'What time is it now?'

'Almost ten,' Donna said.

'Can we do it?'

'All right. Let's get in line.'

They stepped behind the last person in line, a pudgy teenage boy whose hands were folded judiciously across his belly. Without moving his feet, he swivelled enough to cast a critical eye at Donna and Sandy. He made a quiet 'Humph,' as if insulted by their presence, and swung his shoulders towards the front.

'What's *his* problem?' Sandy whispered.

'Shhh.'

Waiting, Donna counted fourteen people in line. Though eight seemed to be children, she only saw two who might qualify for the 'children under twelve' discount. If none of the others had complimentary tickets, she figured the tour would net fifty-two dollars.

Not too shabby, she thought.

The man from the cafe was three from the front.

A young couple with two blond girls stepped up to the ticket booth.

'That makes sixty-four,' Donna said.

'What?'

'Dollars.'

'What time is it?'

'Two minutes to go.'

'I hate waiting.'

'Look at the people.'

'What for?'

'They're interesting.'

Sandy looked up at her mother. Even with sunglasses hiding most of her face, Sandy's scepticism was obvious.

76

But she sidestepped out of line to check the people more closely.

'Fiends!' someone shrieked from behind. 'Ghouls!'

Donna swung around. Crouched in the middle of the street, a thin pale woman pointed at her, at Sandy – at all of them. The woman was no older than thirty. She had the trim, short hair of a boy. Her sleeveless yellow dress was wrinkled and stained. Dirt streaked her white legs. Her feet were bare.

'You and you and you!' she screeched. 'Ghouls! Grave sniffers! Vampires, all of you, sucking the blood of the dead!'

The ticket-booth door slammed open. A man ran out, his gaunt face scarlet. 'Outta here, damn you!'

'Maggots!' she shouted. 'All of you, maggots, paying to see such filth. Vultures! Cowards!'

The man jerked his wide leather belt free of its loops, and doubled it. 'I'm warning you!'

'Corpse fuckers!'

'That about does it,' he muttered.

The woman scampered backward as the man rushed her, belt high and ready. Stumbling, she fell hard on to the pavement. 'Go ahead, maggot! The ghouls love it! Look at 'em gawk. Give 'em blood! That's what they're here for!' Rising to her knees, she ripped open the front of her dress. Her breasts were huge for a woman so small. They swung over her belly like ripe sacks. 'Give 'em a show! Give 'em blood! Tear my flesh! That's what they love!'

He raised the belt overhead, ready to bring it down.

'Don't.' The word shot out, quick and sharp.

The man looked around.

Turning, Donna saw the man from the cafe step out of the line. He walked forward.

'You just stay put, bud.'

He kept walking.

'We don't have need of interference.'

He said nothing to the man with the belt, but walked

past him to the woman. He helped her to her feet. He lifted the dress, covering her shoulders, and pulled it gently shut in front. With a shaking hand, the woman held the torn edges together.

He spoke quietly to her. She thrust herself against him, kissed him wildly on the mouth, and sprang away. 'Run! Run for your lives!' she yelled. 'Run for your souls!' And then she dashed away down the street.

A few people in the crowd laughed. Someone mumbled that the madwoman was part of the show. Others disagreed. The man from the cafe came back and stood silently beside his friend in the line.

'Okay folks!' called the ticket man. He walked towards them, threading his belt through its loops. 'We 'pologize for the delay, though I'm sure we can all appreciate the gal's dilemma. Three weeks back, the beast took her husband and only child, tore 'em to ribbons. The experience unhinged the poor gal. She's been hangin' around here the past couple days, since we started doin' the tours again. But now here's another woman, a woman who passed through the purifyin' fire of tragedy, and came out the better for it. This woman's the owner of Beast House, and your personal guide for today's tour.' With a grand, sweeping gesture, he led the eyes of the crowd towards the lawn of Beast House where a stooped, heavy woman hobbled towards them.

'Do you still want to do it?' Donna asked.

Sandy shrugged. Her face was pale. She had obviously been shocked by the hysterical woman. 'Yeah,' she said, 'I guess so.'

78

# *Chapter Six*

## 1.

They passed through the turnstile, and gathered on the lawn in front of the old woman. She waited, ebony cane planted close to the side of her right foot, her flowered dress blowing lightly against her legs. In spite of the day's warmth, she wore a green silken scarf around her neck. She fingered the scarf briefly, then spoke.

'Welcome to Beast House.' She said it reverently, in a low, husky voice. 'My name's Maggie Kutch, and I own it. I began showing the house to visitors way back in '31, shortly after tragedy took the lives of my husband and three children. You may be asking yourselves why a woman'd want to take people through her home that was a scene of such personal grief. The answer's easy: m-o-n-e-y.'

Quiet laughter stirred through the group. She smiled pleasantly, turned, and limped up the walkway. At the foot of the porch stairs, she wrapped a spotted hand over the newel post and pointed upward with the tip of her cane.

'Here's where they strung up poor Gus Goucher. He was eighteen at the time, and on his way to San Francisco to join his brother working at the Sutro Baths. He stopped here on the afternoon of August 2, 1903, and split firewood for Lilly Thorn, the original owner of the house. She fed him a meal in payment, and Gus was on his way. That very night, the beast struck for the first time. No one, but only Lilly, lived through the attack. She ran into the street screaming as if she'd met the devil himself.

'Right away, the town got up a posse. It searched the house from cellar to attic, but no living thing was found. Only the torn, chewed bodies of Lilly's sister and two little boys. The posse tromped through the wooded hillside yonder and found young Gus Goucher fast asleep.

'Well, some of the townspeople recalled seeing him by the Thorn place that afternoon, and figured this was their man. They gave him a trial. Weren't no witnesses with everybody dead but Lilly, and her raving. They judged him guilty quick enough, though. A mob broke him outta the old jail, that night. They dragged the poor lad to this very spot, whipped a rope over the balcony post up there, and hoisted him.

'Course, Gus Goucher didn't kill no one. It was the beast done it. Let's go in.'

They climbed six wooden stairs to the covered porch.

'You can see this is a new door, here. The original got shot up, three weeks back. You probably saw it on the news. One of our local police shotgunned the door to get inside. He'd of been better off, course, staying out.'

'Tell me,' asked the critical boy, 'how did the Zieglers get inside?'

'They got in like thieves. They broke a window out back.'

'Thank you.' He cast a smile towards the rest of the group, apparently pleased with the service he'd performed.

'Our police,' Maggie Kutch continued, 'spoiled an antique lock we had on the door here. But we did preserve the hinges and the knocker.' She tapped the brass knocker with her cane. 'It's supposed to be the paw of a monkey. Lilly Thorn stuck it here. She was partial to monkeys.'

Maggie opened the door. The group followed her inside. 'One of you get the door, if you would. Don't want the flies to get in.'

She pointed her cane. 'Here's another monkey for you.'

Donna heard her daughter groan, and didn't blame the girl a bit. The stuffed monkey, standing by the wall with its arms out, seemed to be snarling, ready to bite.

'Umbrella stand,' Maggie said. She dropped her cane into the circle of the monkey's arms, then snatched it up again.

'Now I'll show you the scene of the first attack. Right this way, into the parlour.'

Sandy took Donna's hand. Sandy looked up nervously at her mother as they entered a room to the left of the vestibule.

'When I came into this house, way back in '31, it was just the same as Lilly Thorn left it the night of the beast attack twenty-eight years before. Nobody'd lived in the house since then. Nobody'd dared.'

'Why did *you* dare?' asked the chubby, critical boy.

'My husband and I were duped, pure and simple. We were made to believe that poor Gus Goucher did the dirty work on the Thorn people. Nobody let on about no beast.'

Donna glanced at the man from the cafe. He was standing ahead of her, next to his white-haired friend. Donna lifted her hand. 'Mrs Kutch?'

'Yes?'

'Is it definitely known, now, that Gus Goucher was innocent?'

'I don't know how *innocent* he was.'

Some of the people laughed. The man looked around at her. She avoided his eyes.

'He might've been rowdy and a sneak and a no-good. He was surely a stupid man. But everyone in Malcasa Point knew, the minute they clapped eyes on the poor man, that he didn't attack the Thorns.'

'How could they tell?'

'He didn't have claws, sweetie.'

A few in the group tittered. The chubby boy arched an eyebrow at Donna and turned away. The man from the cafe still looked at her. She met his eyes. They held her, penetrated her, set warm fluid spreading in her loins. He didn't look away for a long time. Shaken, Donna tried to recover her composure. She finally returned her attention to the tour.

'. . . through a window out in the kitchen. If you'll just step around the screen here.'

As they moved to the front of a three-panelled papier-mâché screen that partitioned off a corner of the room, someone screamed. Several members of the group gasped with shock. Others mumbled. Some groaned with repugnance. Donna followed her daughter around the screen, glimpsed an outstretched bloody hand on the floor, and stumbled as Sandy bolted back.

Maggie chuckled at the group's reaction.

Donna led Sandy around the end of the screen. Lying on the floor, one leg propped high on the dusty cushion of a couch, was the form of a woman. Her shiny eyes gazed upward. Her bloody face was twisted in a grimace of terror and agony. Tatters of her stained linen gown draped her body, covering little except her breasts and pubic area.

'The beast tore down the screen,' said Maggie, 'and leapt over the back of the couch, taking Ethel Hughes by surprise while she was reading *The Saturday Evening*

*Post*. This is the very magazine she was reading at the time.' Maggie stretched her cane across the body and poked the magazine. 'Everything is just as it was on that awful night.' She smiled pleasantly. 'Except for the body, of course. This replica was created in wax by Mssr Claude Dubois, at my request, way back in 1936. Every detail is guaranteed authentic, down to the tiniest bite mark on her poor neck. We used morgue photos.

'Of course, this is the gown that Ethel actually wore that night. These dark places are made by her blood.'

'Was there sexual assault?' the white-haired man asked in a strained voice.

Magie's pleasant eyes hardened, flicking towards his face. 'No,' she said.

'That's not what I heard.'

'I can't be responsible for what you heard, sir. I only know what I know, and I know more about the beast of this house than any other person, living or dead. The beast of this house has never carnally abused its victims.'

'Then I apologize,' he said in a cold voice.

'When the beast was done with Ethel, it rampaged through the parlour. It knocked this alabaster bust of Caesar off the mantle, breaking the nose.' The nose rested on the fireplace mantle beside the bust. 'It dashed half a dozen figurines into the fireplace. It upset chairs. This fine rosewood pedestal table was thrown through the bay window. The racket, of course, awakened the rest of the household. Lilly's room was right up there.' Maggie pointed towards the high ceiling with her cane. 'The beast must've heard her stirring. It went for the stairs.'

Silently, she led the group out of the parlour and up a broad stairway to the second floor hall. They turned to the left. Maggie stepped through a side doorway and into a bedroom.

'We're now above the parlour. Here's where Lilly Thorn was sleeping the night of the beast attack.' A wax figure, dressed in a lacy pink gown, was sitting upright, staring fearfully over the brass scrollwork at the foot of the bed. 'When the commotion woke Lilly up, she dragged the dressing table from there' – she pointed her cane at the heavy rosewood table and mirror beside the window – 'to there, barricading the door. Then she made her escape through the window. She jumped to the roof of the bay window below, then to the ground.

'It's always been a wonder to me that she didn't try to save her children.'

They followed Maggie out of the bedroom.

'When the beast found that he couldn't get into her room, he came down the hall this way.'

They passed the top of the stairs. Ahead, four Brentwood chairs blocked the centre of the corridor. Clothesline was strung from one chair to the next, closing off the centre space. The members of the group squeezed between one of the lines and the wall.

'This is where we'll put our new display. The figures are already on order, but we don't expect to have them much before spring.'

'That's a shame,' the man with the two children told his wife in a sarcastic voice.

Maggie entered a door to the right. 'The beast found this door open,' she said.

The windows of the room faced the wooded hillside behind the house. The room's two brass beds looked much like the one in Lilly's room, but the covers were heaped in disarray. A rocking horse with faded paint stood in one corner, next to the wash stand.

'Earl was ten,' Maggie said. 'His brother, Sam, was eight.'

Their wax bodies, torn and chewed, lay sprawled face down between the two beds. Both wore the remains of striped nightshirts that concealed little except their buttocks.

'Let's go,' said the man with the two children. 'This is the most crude, tasteless excuse for a voyeuristic thrill I've ever come across.'

His wife smiled apologetically at Maggie.

'Twelve bucks for this!' the man spat. 'Good God!' His wife and children followed him out of the room.

A trim woman in a white blouse and shorts took her teenage son by the elbow. 'We're going, too.'

'Mother!'

'No argument. We've both seen too much already.'

'Aw geez!'

She tugged him out the door.

When they were gone, Maggie laughed quietly. 'They left before we got to the best part,' she said.

Nervous laughter whispered through the remaining members of the group.

## 2.

'We lived sixteen nights in this house before the beast struck.' She led them through the corridor, past the blocking chairs and past the stairway. 'My husband, Joseph, he had a distaste for the rooms where the murders happened. That's partly why we left 'em well enough alone, and settled ourselves elsewhere. Cynthia and Diana weren't so squeamish. They stayed in the boys' room we just left.'

She took the group through a doorway on the right, across from Lilly's bedroom. Donna hunted the floor for wax bodies, but found none, though a four-panelled papier-mâché screen blocked one corner and window.

'Joseph and I were sleeping here. The night was the seventh of May 1931. That's more than forty years back, but it's burned in my mind. There'd been a good deal of rain that day. It slowed down after dark. We had those windows open. I could hear the drizzle outside. The girls were fast asleep at the end of the hall, and the baby, Theodore, was snug in the nursery.

'I fell asleep, feeling all peaceful and safe. But long about midnight, I was awakened by a loud crash of glass. The sound came from downstairs. Joseph, who also heard it, got up real quiet and tiptoed over here to the chest. He always kept his pistol here.' Opening a top drawer, she pulled out a Colt .45 service automatic. '*This* pistol. It made a frightful loud sound when he worked its top.' Clamping her cane under one arm, she gripped the black hood of the automatic and quickly slid it back and forward with a scraping clamour of metal parts. Her thumb gently lowered the hammer. She returned the gun to its drawer.

'Joseph took the pistol with him and left the room. When I heard his footsteps on the stairs, I stole out of bed, myself. Quiet as I could, I started down the hall. I had to get to my children, you see.'

The group followed her into the corridor.

'I was right here, at the top of the stairway, when I heard gunshots from downstairs. I heard a scream from Joseph such as I'd never heard before. There were sounds of a scuffle, then scampering feet. I stood right here, scared frozen, listening to footsteps climb the stairs. I wanted to run off, and take my children to safety, but fear held me tight so I couldn't move.

'Out of the darkness below me came the beast. I couldn't see how it looked, except it walked upright like a man. It made kind of a laugh, and then it leapt on me and dragged me down to the floor. It ripped me with its claws and teeth. I tried to fight it off, but of course I was no match for the thing. I was preparing myself to meet the Lord when little Theodore started crying in his nursery at the end of the hall. The beast climbed off me and ran to the nursery.

'Wounded as I was, I chased after it. I *had* to save my baby.'

The group followed her to the end of the corridor. Maggie stopped in front of a closed door.

'This door stood open,' she said, and tapped it with her cane. 'In the light from its windows I saw the pale beast drag my child from the cradle and fall upon him.

I knew that little Theodore was beyond my power to help him.

'I was watching, filled with horror, when a hand tugged at my nightdress. I found Cynthia and Diana behind me, all in tears. I took a hand of each, and led them silently away from the nursery door.'

She took the group again past the rope-connected chairs.

'We were just here when the snarling beast ran out of the nursery. This was the nearest door.' She opened it, revealing a steep, narrow staircase with a door at the top. 'We ducked inside, and I got the door shut only a second ahead of the beast. The three of us ran up these stairs as fast as our legs could carry us, stumbling and crying out in the darkness. At the top, we passed through that door. I bolted it after us. Then we sat in the musty blackness of the attic, waiting.

'We heard the beast come up the stairs. It made laughing, hissing sounds. It sniffed the door. And then, somehow, with such quickness we couldn't move, the door burst open and the beast sprang among us. In the first moments, it killed Cynthia and Diana. Then it leapt on to me. It held me down with its claws, and I waited for it to tear out my life. But it didn't. It just stayed on top of me, breathing its foul breath against my face. Then it climbed off. It scampered down the attic and vanished. I have never seen the beast since that night. But others have.'

3.

'Why didn't it kill you?' asked the girl whose round face bloomed with acne.

'I've often wondered that. Though I'll never know, this side of the grave, I sometimes think the beast let me stay alive "to report its cause aright to the unsatisfied," as the dying Hamlet asked Horatio to do. Maybe it didn't want another Gus Goucher strung up for its crimes.'

'It seems to me,' said the white-haired man, 'that you give this beast a great deal of credit.'

'Let's see the attic,' said the chubby, critical boy.

'I don't show the attic. I keep it locked – always.'

'The nursery, then.'

'I never show that, either.'

'You don't have more dummies?'

'There're no wax figures of my kin,' she said.

With arched eyebrows, the boy scanned the group as if looking for others who shared his disdain for the woman's selective presentation of history. 'Well, what about those other two guys? They weren't your kin.'

'The *two guys* this young man refers to, they're Tom Bagley and Larry Maywood.' She shut the door to the attic staircase and led the group back down the corridor to her bedroom. 'Tom and Larry were twelve years old. I knew both of them well. They came along on several tours, and probably knew more about Beast House than just about anyone.

'Lord knows why they didn't have more sense than to come in here at night. They weren't ignorant like those Ziegler characters: they knew good and well what to expect. But they come breaking in, anyhow. This was back in '51.

'They were in the house a long spell, nosing around. They tried to pick the locks of the nursery and attic, but couldn't. They were snooping through this room when the beast came.

'It took down little Tom Bagley, and Larry Maywood ran for the window.'

Maggie pulled aside the papier-mâché screen that blocked the window and several feet of floor space in front of it. Some of the group jumped back. The girl with acne whirled away, gagging. A woman muttered, 'Really,' her voice rich with disgust.

The wax figure of Larry Maywood, trying to raise the

window, was looking back at the same mangled body as the other spectators in the room. Its clothes were shredded, leaving it bare except for the buttocks. The skin of its back was deeply scored. Its head lay half a foot from the pulpy neck, face up, eyes open, mouth twisted wide.

'Leaving his friend at the mercy of the beast, Larry Maywood jumped from . . .'

'I'm Larry Maywood!' cried the white-haired man. 'And you are lying! Tommy was dead! He was dead before I jumped. I saw the beast twist off his head! I'm no coward! I didn't leave him there to die!'

Sandy squeezed Donna's hand tightly.

One of the children began to cry.

'This is slander! Out-and-out slander!' Spinning away, the man marched out of the room. His friend from the cafe followed.

'I've seen about enough,' Donna whispered.

'Me too.'

'That concludes our tour for this morning, ladies and gentlemen.' Maggie left the room, followed by the group. 'We do have a gift shop on the first floor, where you can purchase an illustrated booklet on the history of Beast House. You can also purchase 35 mm colour slides of the house, including the murder scenes. We have Beast House T-shirts, bumper stickers, and all sorts of fine souvenirs. The Ziegler display will be ready next spring. You won't want to miss it.'

# Chapter Seven

## 1.

'Imagine the gall of that hag, suggesting I ran out on Tommy to save my own skin! That miserable bag of guts, that abomination! I'll take legal action!'

'I wish you hadn't leaked your identity.'

'Well, I'm sorry.' He shook his head, frowning in misery. 'But *really*, Judge, you heard what she said about me.'

'I heard.'

'The contemptible vial of swamp gas!'

'Excuse me!' a woman's voice called from behind.

'Oh dear,' Larry muttered.

They looked around at the woman hurrying up the sidewalk towards them, a blond girl in tow. Jud recognized them both.

'We'll make a run for the car,' Larry whispered.

'I don't think that's necessary.'

'Judge, please! She's undoubtedly a reporter or some other species of uncouth snoop.'

'She looks couth to me.'

'Oh for heaven's sake!' He stamped his foot. 'Please!'

'You go to the car, and I'll check her out.' Jud held out the keys. Larry snatched them away and hurried off several paces ahead of the woman. 'He has a healthy fear of the press,' Jud told her.

'I'm not the press,' she said.

'I didn't think so.'

She smiled.

'But if you're not the press, why did you chase us?'

'Afraid you'd get away.'

'Oh?'

'Yes.' Head tilted to one side, she shrugged. 'I'm Donna Hayes.' She offered a hand. Jud held it lightly. 'This is my daughter, Sandy.'

'I'm Jud Rucker,' he said, still holding her hand. 'What can I do for you?'

'We saw you at breakfast.'

'*I* didn't,' Sandy said.

'Well, I did.'

Jud frowned, enjoying himself and still holding her hand. 'Oh yes,' he finally said. 'You were at the table behind me, weren't you?'

Donna nodded. 'We were on the tour, too.'

'Right. Did you enjoy it?'

'*I* thought it was dreadful.'

'*I* liked it,' the girl said. 'It was so gross.'

'It was gross, all right.' He turned his eyes to Donna and stayed quiet, waiting.

'Anyway,' she said. She took a deep breath. In spite of her smile, she looked worried.

'How'd you like that crazy woman before the tour?' Sandy asked him.

The worry suddenly vanished from Donna's face. In a voice thick with sincerity, she said, 'That's why I wanted to see you, why I ... chased you the way I did.' She smiled shyly. 'I wanted to tell you how refreshing it was, the way you stuck up for that woman. The way you helped her. It was such a thoughtful thing to do.'

'Thank you.'

'You should've given that turkey a knuckle sandwich,' Sandy told him.

'I gave the matter lots of thought.'

'You should've punched out his lights.'

'He backed off.'

'Sandy has a taste for violence,' Donna said.

'Well,' said Jud. He let the single word stand like a period, ending his part of the conversation.

'Well,' Donna echoed. Though she kept her smile, Jud could see her start to deflate. 'I just wanted to let you know . . . how much I admired the way you helped the woman.'

'Thank you. Nice to meet both of you.'

'Nice to meet you,' Sandy said.

Donna started to pull her hand away, but Jud tightened his grip. 'Do you have time for a Bloody Mary?' he asked.

'Well . . .'

'Sandy,' he said, 'how about a Coke or 7-up?'

'Sure!'

'How about it?' he asked Donna.

'Sure. Why not?'

'I think the Welcome Inn should have what we're looking for. Are you on foot?'

'We've been on them all morning,' said Donna.

'In that case, I'll personally chauffeur you to the door.' He walked beside them to his Chrysler, and found it locked. Larry grinned out at him, brimming with satisfaction. Jud made a cranking motion. With a humming sound, the passenger window opened.

'Yes?' Larry asked innocently.

'They're friends.'

'Maybe *your* friends.'

Jud turned to Donna. 'Charm him.'

93

She bent beside the car. At eye level with him, she said, 'I'm Donna Hayes.' She reached a hand into the window. Larry met it with his hand and shook it briefly, making a smile that seemed to strain his face.

'Admit it,' he said. 'You're a reporter.'

'I'm a passenger-service agent with TWA.'

'You're not.'

'I am.'

'She is,' said Sandy.

'Who asked you?' he snapped.

Sandy began to giggle.

'Who's she?'

'That's Sandy, my daughter.'

'Daughter, eh? Then you're married?'

'Not anymore.'

'Ah-ha! A feminist!'

Sandy turned away, laughing out of control.

'Don't you like feminists?' Donna asked him.

'Only with Béarnaise sauce,' he said.

When Donna laughed, the corners of Larry's mouth began to tremble with concealed mirth. 'I suppose . . .' He swallowed. 'I suppose I'll be relegated to the back seat with Little Miss Giggles.' He unlocked the door and climbed out.

Donna stepped into the car. She scooted to the middle of the front seat. 'Miss Giggles can manage the back seat on her own.'

'A *lady!* I've met a *lady!*' Larry got in beside her. She unlocked the driver's door for Jud, while Larry reached behind him to get the lock of the back door.

'Where to?' Larry asked, slapping his thighs.

'The Welcome Inn,' said Jud. 'For drinks and lunch.'

'Wonderful. A party. I love parties.' He looked over his shoulder. 'Don't you love parties, Miss Giggles?'

'I find them enchanting,' replied Sandy, and burst into a new fit of hysteria.

As they were passing the Chevron station, Sandy called out, 'There's our car!'

94

'Is it sick?' Larry asked.

Donna said, 'We had a little accident last night.'

'Nothing serious, I hope.'

'Just bruises and scrapes.'

'Would you like me to stop?' Jud asked.

'Would you mind?'

He pulled into the station. Larry climbed out to let Donna through. Then he got back in and shut the door.

'I suppose it's never difficult for a woman to demolish a car,' Larry said, looking around at the girl. 'How did your mother accomplish it?'

Jud didn't listen to the girl's reply. All his attention was focused on Donna: on the way the sun shimmered in the flow of her brown hair, on the inward curve of her back and how the mounds of her buttocks shifted under her corduroy pants as she walked. In front of the office, she met a man wearing coveralls and a smirk. They talked. Donna tossed her rump to the left and slid a hand down her rear pocket. She nodded. With a graceful pivot, she followed the man to her car, where he opened the hood and shook his head.

Jud watched her hair sweep down the side of her face as she ducked to look under the hood. She straightened up, talking.

'Uh-oh,' he heard Sandy say.

The man slammed the hood shut.

Donna talked to him, and nodded while he spoke. She pushed both hands into her hip pockets, and shifted again to her left leg. Then she swung around. She walked with long strides towards Jud's car, shrugged, made a face to show exasperation, and smiled.

Larry climbed out to let her in.

'Well,' she told Jud, 'it's still among the living. He has to send to Santa Rosa, though, for a new radiator.'

'It'll take a couple of days, won't it?'

'He said we might be able to leave tomorrow.'

'Tomorrow?' Sandy sounded worried.

'There's no way around it, honey.'

'Do you need to get somewhere in a hurry?' Jud asked, and pulled on to the road.

'No, not especially. Two days in this town is just about two days longer than we'd planned on, that's all.'

'I spent twelve years in this marvellous berg,' said Larry. 'You'd be amazed at the variety of activities available to you.'

'What sort of things?' asked Sandy.

'The most popular sport, by far, is sitting at the corner of Front and Division to watch the traffic lights change.'

'Oh boy.'

'Do you have a place to stay?' Jud asked.

Donna nodded. 'We've got a room at the Welcome Inn.'

'Why, isn't that a joyful coincidence!' Larry proclaimed. 'So do we! Do all of us play bridge?'

'Never touch the stuff,' Jud said.

'Don't *brag!*'

'Besides, we've already got plans for tonight.'

'Oh.'

'We have some business to take care of,' he told Donna.

'Are you just in town for today?' she asked.

'We may be around for a few days. It's hard to say, at this point. Depends on how things go.'

'What sort of business are you in?'

'We're with . . .' He suddenly knew that he didn't want to lie. Not to this woman. The need to retain a cover wasn't as great as usual, and not worth the loss. 'I'd rather not go into it,' he said.

'Oh. Fine. I'm sorry if I pried.'

'No, don't . . .'

'I'd be happy to tell you our business.'

'Larry!'

'We're going to . . .'

'Don't!'

'Kill the beast.'

'What?' Donna asked.

'Wow!' cried Sandy.

'The beast. The monster of Beast House. Judgement Rucker and I are going to lay it low!'

'Are you?' Donna asked, turning to Jud.

'Do you believe there is a beast?' he asked.

'Something killed all those people, I guess.'

'Or some*one*,' Jud said.

'The killer of Tom Bagley was *not* human,' Larry insisted.

'What was it?' asked Sandy.

'We'll show you its cadaver,' Larry said, 'and you may decide for yourself.'

'What's a cadaver?'

'It's a corpse, honey.'

'Oh, gross.'

'What we plan to do,' Jud said, 'is find out what – or who – killed the people in that house. Then we'll deal with it.' He smiled at her. 'Bet you didn't realize you were riding with a couple of lunatics. Are you still up to a Bloody Mary?'

'Now I may need two.'


## 2.


'Excuse me,' Donna said. She scooted back her chair. 'If the drinks come while I'm gone, don't wait on me.'

'I'll come, too,' said the girl.

Jud watched them walk across the crowded dining room. Then he leaned close to Larry. In a low voice, he said, 'You screwed up real good, back there. If one more person finds out what we're doing in this town, it's all over. I keep my advance, drive back to San Francisco, and that's the end of it.'

'*Really*, Judge. What possible harm . . .?'

'One more person.'

'Oh, all right. If you must be that way.'

'I must.'

Nobody spoke of Beast House during cocktails or lunch. As they were finishing, Larry told of a footpath that led down a gorge to a beach.

After lunch, they all went to the motel office and registered for another night. Then the two groups split up, giving Donna and Sandy a chance to put on their swimsuits. Jud relaxed on his bed, ankles crossed, hands folded behind his head. He fell asleep.

'There they are!' Larry announced, waking him. The nervous man left the window and inspected himself in a mirror over the dressing table. 'How do I look?'

Jud glanced at the red-flowered shirt and white shorts. 'Where's your Panama hat?'

'I could hardly pack everything on such short notice.'

They left their cabin. Larry rushed ahead to meet the two women, but Jud hung back to have a long look at Donna. She wore a blue shirt with sleeves rolled up her forearms. Below the hanging shirt tails, her legs were slim and dark. No trace of a swimsuit was visible.

'I do hope you're not *au naturel* under that blouse,' Larry said.

'You'll have to wait and see.'

'Oh please, give us a peek. Just a teensy one.'

'Nope.'

'Oh please.'

Sandy lunged forward laughing, and swung her denim handbag at Larry. He spun away, ducking. The bag whunked his back. 'Cruel midget!' he cried out.

The girl started to swing again.

'That's enough, honey.'

'But he's weird,' Sandy gasped, laughing.

'Is he always this way?' Donna asked Jud.

'I only met him last night.'

'Is that true?'

'Judgement never lies,' Larry said.

They got into Jud's Chrysler, and Larry gave directions that took them down Front Street past the Chevron station, past Sarah's Diner, and down two more blocks

98

of shops. Beast House loomed ahead, on the left. The talking and laughter abruptly stopped, but nobody mentioned the house.

Larry broke the silence. 'Turn right on this dirt road.'

Jud made the turn.

'Is that where Axel's mother lives?' Sandy asked, pointing to the brick house.

'That's the place,' said Donna.

Jud looked at the brick house to his left and saw that it had no windows. 'Strange,' he muttered.

'Indeed,' said Larry. He asked Donna, 'How do you know Axel?'

'He gave us a ride into town last night.'

'There's a weird duck.'

'He's retarded,' Sandy explained.

'Who wouldn't be, with a mother like Maggie Kutch?'

'What?' asked Sandy.

'Axel's mother is Maggie Kutch, the owner of Beast House, the tour guide.'

'Her?'

'Yes indeed.'

'Did she remarry after the killings?' Donna asked.

'Keep to the right, Judge. No, she did have visitors, though. Town speculation had it that Wick Hapson fathered Axel. He's been working with Maggie from the start, and they live together.'

'The man in the ticket booth?' Donna asked.

'Right-o.'

'Charming family,' Jud said. 'It looked like the house didn't have any windows.'

'It doesn't.'

'How come?' Sandy asked.

'So the beast can't get in, of course.'

'Oh.' The girl sounded as if she regretted asking.

The dirt road widened and ended.

'Ah, we're here! Just park anywhere, Judge.'

He turned the car around so it headed out, and parked off to the side of the road.

'You'll absolutely adore this beach,' Larry said, getting out.

Before opening his door, Jud watched Donna. As he'd assumed, she was wearing a swimsuit under the shirt: the bottom part of one, at least. Its blue fabric shined at him when she bent to climb out.

He joined the others beside the car. The wind felt good, cutting the heat like a cool spray.

'Are we off?' Larry asked Donna.

'We off?' she asked Jud.

'I'm ready. You ready, Sandy?'

'You're *all* weird.'

They walked single file along a narrow trail that angled downward between two sandy hills. Jud squinted into the wind. It fluttered in his ears, batting away all but the loudest words as Larry told of a childhood experience at the beach.

After they rounded a curve in the trail, the ocean came into view. Its choppy blue was frothing with rows of whitecaps. Waves slammed against a rocky point. Just this side of the point, the waves washed quietly on to a stretch of sand. Jud could see nobody down there.

'Ah wonderful!' Larry yelled, spreading his arms and sniffing a deep breath. 'Last one to the beach is a rotten egg!' He began to run. Sandy chased after him.

Jud turned to Donna. 'Don't you feel like racing?'

'Nope.' Wind threw strands of hair across her face. Jud brushed them away. He couldn't look away from her eyes.

'I bet I know why,' he said.

'Why?'

'You're afraid I'll beat you.'

'Is that it?' Her eyes were amused, but serious, as if she wouldn't permit herself to be distracted by his banter.

'That's it,' he said.

'Is your name really Judgement?'

'It really is.'

100

'I wish we were alone, Judgement.'

He put his hands on her shoulders and drew her against him, feeling the press of her body, the light touch of her hands against his back, the smooth, moist opening of her lips.

'We're not alone,' she said after a while.

'I guess we'd better quit, huh?'

'While the quitting's good.'

'I wouldn't say it's good,' Jud said.

'Me neither.'

Holding hands, they walked down the trail. Below, Sandy was running across the beach just ahead of Larry. She splashed into the water. Larry stopped at the water's edge and dropped to his knees. The girl waved for him to come in, but he shook his head. 'Come on!' Jud heard through the noise of the wind and surf.

Sandy pranced in the water, crouched and splashed at Larry.

'We'd better hurry,' Donna said, 'before my charming daughter gets carried away and drags him in.'

Even as she said it, the girl ran ashore and began to tug one of Larry's arms.

'Leave him alone, Sandy!'

Larry, still on his knees, managed to look around. 'It's really all right, Donna,' he called. 'She's nothing I can't handle.'

Letting go of his arm, Sandy circled behind him and leapt on to his back. 'Giddyap!' she shouted.

He lunged and twisted, scrambling through the sand on hands and knees, making a noise that sounded, at first, like the whinny of a horse. Then he was on his feet. Sandy, clutching him tightly around the neck, looked back at Donna and Jud. Though she said nothing, her face showed fear. Larry swung himself in a circle, tugging at the girl's arms, and Jud saw terror in his wide eyes. His whinnies were ragged gasps of panic. He pranced and bucked, trying to tear himself free.

'Oh my God!' Donna cired, and broke into a run.

Jud raced past her towards the girl now screaming in horror.

'Larry, stop!' he yelled.

The man didn't seem to hear. He kept jumping and writhing, pulling frantically at the girl's arms.

Then Sandy was falling backward, her legs still hugging Larry's hips but her arms loose and flailing. One of her small hands clutched Larry's collar. The shirt split down his back, and he screamed. Jud caught the falling girl. He pulled her free.

Larry spun, looking at them, his eyes wild. He began backing away. He fell. Propping himself on an elbow, he still gazed at them. Slowly, the strangeness left his face. His harsh breathing grew calm.

Jud left Sandy in her mother's arms and went to him.

'She shouldn't . . . have jumped on my back.' His voice was a high whine. 'Not on my *back*.'

'It's all right now,' Jud said.

'Not on my back.' He lay on the sand, covering his eyes with his forearms, and wept silently.

Jud knelt beside him. 'It's all right, Larry. It's all over.'

'It's not over. It'll never be over. Never.'

'You gave the kid a terrible scare.'

'I kno-o-o-w,' he said, stretching the word like a groan of misery. 'I'm sor-ry. Maybe . . . if I apologize.'

'Might help.'

He sniffed, and wiped his eyes. When he sat up, Jud saw the scars. They criss-crossed his shoulders and back in a savage tracery more white than his pale skin.

'They're not from the beast, if that's what you think. I got them from my fall. The beast never touched me. Never.'

# Chapter Eight

Roy made certain, once again, that Joni was securely tied. Probably it didn't matter. She'd obviously lost her marbles. But Roy wanted nothing left to chance.

In the living room, he bent down and lit the candle. He patted the newspaper wads to make certain, once again, they were touching the candle stick. Then he headed for the kitchen, stepping high, his feet crushing the newspaper wads and clothes he'd scattered along the floor.

The fire might not destory all the evidence, but it couldn't hurt.

He put on sunglasses and a faded Dodger cap that had belonged to Marv, and went out the back door. Pulling it shut, he twisted his hand to smear prints on the knob. He trotted down three steps to the patio, then hurried to the driveway. Looking towards the street, he saw that a gate blocked the driveway. He walked casually to it, unlatched it, and opened it.

The neighbour's house was very close. He watched its windows, but saw nobody looking out.

He walked up the driveway to the garage. A two-car garage, with two doors separated by a beam. He raised the left-hand door. Inside was a red Chevy. He climbed into it, glanced at the three sets of keys he'd brought from the house, and easily found the Chevrolet keys.

He started the car and backed out of the garage. He stopped close to the kitchen door. Then he got out and opened the trunk. He brought Joni out of the house, set her inside the trunk, and slammed the lid shut.

The trip to Karen's house took less than ten minutes. He'd expected to recognize the house, but it didn't look familiar at all. He checked the address again. Then he remembered that she and Bob moved just before the trial. This was the right house.

He parked in front. He checked his wristwatch – Marv's wristwatch – his now. Nearly two-thirty.

The neighbourhood seemed very quiet. He looked up and down the block as he walked to the front door. Four houses to the right, a Japanese gardener was whacking limbs from a bush. To the left, a lawn away, a lone tabby cat crouched, stalking something. Roy didn't bother trying to spot its prey. He had some prey of his own.

Grinning, he rang the doorbell. He waited, and rang again. Finally he decided nobody was in.

He headed around the side of the house, took two steps past the rear corner, and stopped abruptly.

There she was. Maybe not Karen, but *some* woman on a chaise longue, listening to music from a transistor radio. The longue was facing away, so its back blocked Roy's view of all but her slim, tanned legs, her left arm, and the crown of her hat. A white hat, like a sailor's.

Roy scanned the yard. High shrubbery enclosed its sides and rear. Good and secluded. Bending low, he raised his pants leg and slipped the knife from its sheath.

Silently, he stepped closer until he could see over the back of the longue. The woman was wearing a white bikini, its straps hanging off her shoulders. Her skin was glossy with oil. She held a folded magazine in her right hand, keeping it off to the side so it wouldn't cast a shadow on her belly.

Her hand jerked, dropping the magazine as Roy clutched her mouth.

He pressed the knife edge to her throat.

'Don't make a sound, or I'll open you up.'

She tried to say something through his hand.

'Shut up. I'm gonna take my hand away, and you're not gonna make a sound. Ready?'

Her head nodded once.

Roy let go of her mouth, flung the sailor's hat off her head, and clutched her brown hair. 'Okay, stand up.' He helped by pulling her hair. When she was up, he jerked her head around. The tanned face belonged to Karen, all right. He could tell that, even through the sunglasses. 'Not a word,' he muttered.

He guided her to the back door.

'Open it,' he said.

She pulled open the screen door. They stepped into the kitchen. It seemed very dark after the sunny yard, but Roy couldn't spare a hand to take off his sunglasses. 'I need rope,' he said. 'Where do you keep it?'

'You mean I'm allowed to talk now?'

'Where's some rope?'

'We don't have any.'

He put pressure on the blade. 'You'd better hope you do. Now, where is it?'

'I don't . . .' She gasped as he yanked her hair. 'We have some with the camping gear, I think.'

'Show me.' He lifted the knife off her throat, but kept it half an inch away, his wrist propped on her shoulder. 'Move.'

They went out the kitchen, and turned left down a hallway. They walked past closed doors: closets, probably. Past the bathroom. Into a doorway on the right. The room was a study with bookshelves, a cluttered desk, a rocking chair.

'Any kids?' Roy asked.

'No.'

'Too bad.'

She stopped at a door beside the rocker. 'In there,' she said.

'Open it.'

She pulled open the door. The closet held nothing but camping gear: two mummy bags suspended from hangers, hiking boots on the floor, backpacks propped against the wall. A metal-tipped walking stick hung from a hook. Beside it were two soft felt hats. Yellow foam-rubber pads, strapped neatly into rolls, stood upright beside the packs. On the shelf was a long red stuffbag, probably containing a mountain tent. On hangers were outdoor clothes: rain ponchos, flannel shirts, even a pair of grey leather Liederhosen.

'Where's the rope?'

'In the packs.'

He let go of her hair. He took the knife away from her throat and touched the point to her bare back. 'Get it.'

She stepped into the closet and knelt down. She flipped back the red cover of a Kelty pack. She tipped the pack forward, reaching into it, and rummaged through it. Her hand came out with a coil of stiff, new clothesline.

'Is there more?' He took it from her and tossed it behind him.

'Isn't that enough?'

'Look in the other pack.'

She turned to it without closing the first one. As she peeled back its cover, her arm seemed to freeze.

'Don't.' Roy slipped the blade through Karen's hair

106

until its point stopped against the back of her neck. She sucked a quick breath. Keeping the knife at her neck, Roy bent down. He reached over her shoulder and lifted the hand axe out of the pack. Its haft was wood. A leather case enclosed its head. He tossed the axe behind him. It thumped heavily on the carpeted floor.

'Okay, now get the other rope.'

She searched inside the pack and brought out a coil of clothesline much like the first, but grey and soft with wear.

'Get up.'

She stood.

Roy swung her around to face him. 'Hands out.' He pulled the rope away from her. He slid his knife under his belt and tightly bound her hands together. He stepped away from her, paying out rope. Then he picked up the hand axe and the spare coil. Pulling the rope, he led her out the doorway and into the hall. He found the master bedroom at the end of the hall. He pulled her into it.

'Guess what happens now,' he said.

'Aren't I too old for you?'

He grinned, remembering Joni. 'You're way too old for me,' he said. He led her across the carpeted room to a closet. He opened its door halfway and shoved Karen against the wall. With the door between them, he passed the rope over its top and pulled.

'Damn it!' she muttered.

'Shut up.'

'Roy!'

He yanked the rope. The door knocked against him as Karen hit its other side. He saw her fingertips over its top. No doorknob on the inside. Shit! He ran the taut line down to the bottom of the door. Crawling, he brought it under the edge to the front. He lifted one of Karen's feet. She kicked at him. He punched her behind the knee, making her cry out. Then he brought the rope up between her legs and crossed it over her right leg. He tied it to the knob, next to her hip.

He stepped back and admired his work. Karen stood pressed to the door, arms stretched to the top. The rope appeared at the bottom of the door, near the centre, and angled to the right, passing over her leg to the doorknob.

'Now tell me what I want to know.'

'What's that?'

'Where're Donna and Sandy?'

'At their place?' she asked. In spite of her situation, her voice maintained a sarcastic edge.

Roy sliced through one shoulder strap of her bikini, then the other. 'They aren't there, and you know it.'

'They aren't?'

He cut through its back. He reached to her side, and tugged the bikini top from between her body and the door. 'Tell me where they are.'

'If they aren't at home, I wouldn't . . .'

He sliced through the left side of her bikini pants. The edges flopped away. She clamped her legs shut to keep the pants from slipping down.

'What time does your husband get home?'

'Soon.'

'What time?' He pulled the pants down to her ankles.

'Maybe four-thirty.'

'It's only three now. That gives us lots of time.'

'I don't know where they went.'

'Oh?' He laughed. 'You may be able to take a lot of pain. I'll be happy to give it to you. But let me tell you something: if you love that husband of yours, you'll tell me what I want to know before he gets home. When you tell me where they are, I'll leave. I won't hurt you, I won't hurt your husband. If I'm still here when he gets home, though, I'm going to kill you and him both.'

'I don't *know* where she is.'

'Sure you do.'

'I don't.'

'Well then, that's too bad for both of you, isn't it?'

She said nothing.

'Where did they go?'

Crouching, he drew a question mark on the white flesh of her left buttock, and watched it bleed.

# *Chapter Nine*

## 1.

From his position on Front Street near the south corner of the wrought-iron fence, Jud watched half a dozen people leave Beast House. The final tour of the day was over. He looked at his wristwatch. Almost four.

Maggie Kutch left the house last, and locked the door. She made her way slowly down the porch steps, leaning heavily on her cane. The strain of guiding tourists showed plainly in the weariness of her walk.

At the ticket booth, she met Wick Hapson. They finished locking up. Then, taking her arm, Wick walked with her across Front Street. They went slowly up the dirt driveway and finally disappeared into the window-less house.

Jud slid a cigar out of his shirt pocket. He tore the wrapper off, crumbled it into a tiny ball, and flipped it onto the car floor. Then he took a book of matches from the same pocket. He lit the cigar and waited.

At four twenty-five, and old pick-up truck backed out of the garage beside the Kutch house and came down the driveway trailing a cloud of dust. It turned on to Front Street and headed towards Jud. He pretended to study a road map. The truck slowed and swung across the street.

Looking up from his map, Jud saw a man leap to the ground and hobble towards the fence. At the corner was a wide gate, chained shut and padlocked. The short, heavy man opened the lock, unwound the chain, and pushed the gate open. He drove through, then locked the gate again.

Jud watched the truck move over tyre tracks worn into the lawn, and park at the side of Beast House. The driver climbed out. He let down the truck's tailgate and hopped into its bed. Bending down, he slid a board ramp to the ground. Then he rolled a power lawnmower down the ramp.

As soon as the man started the mower, Jud made a U-turn. He drove slowly, studying the left side of the road. Two miles south of Malcasa Point, he found a fire road leading into the forest. Nothing closer. It was no good. He used it to turn around, and headed back toward town.

A hundred yards behind the spot where he'd parked to watch the house front, he pulled completely off the road. He got out of his car. Nothing was in sight except the bending road and wooded slopes. He stood motionless for a few seconds, making sure.

He heard the far-off motor of the lawnmower. He heard the wind stirring leaves high overhead, and the sounds of countless birds. A fly buzzed near his face. He waved it away and opened the trunk of his car.

He put on the parka, first. Then he hooked a web belt around his waist under the coat, and made sure the holster flap was snapped shut. He lifted out a backpack, and put it on. He took out his rifle case. Then he shut the trunk.

His trek through the pathless woods took him up the side of a hill, over rock clusters and fallen trees, and finally into the sunlight of a clearing at the top. He rubbed sweat out of his stinging eyes. He drank tepid water from his canteen. Then he started down the left side of the hill, seeking an outcropping of rock that he'd noticed that morning through the back windows of Beast House.

He finally saw the rocks ahead. He made his way forward and easily climbed the outcropping, hopping from one rock to the next. When he peered over the top, a clear view of Beast House lay below him.

The short, limping man, apparently finished with the front lawn, was now mowing the back. Jud watched him slowly walk the yard, disappear behind a weathered gazebo, and reappear.

It would be a long wait.

But he didn't intend to do it this way, crouched and peeking over a ledge of rock. Too damned uncomfortable. He backed off. He found a level area between a pair of midget pines several feet from the top. There he set down his rifle case. He shrugged the pack off his shoulders and propped it against one of the pines. Then he removed his coat. The breeze cooled his sweaty shirt. He took the shirt off, used it to wipe his face, and spread it out on a rock to let the sun dry it.

Next, he opened his pack. He pulled out his binoculars case, and a sandwich from a paper bag. Donna had made the sandwich for him earlier in the afternoon. They'd returned to the Welcome Inn after the scene with Larry at the beach. Donna and Sandy had changed out of their swimsuits, and Larry had wandered off, presumably to have a drink in the motel bar. Then Jud, accompanied by the two women, had walked into town. He bought the sandwich ingredients at a grocery store near Sarah's Diner. Back in Donna's cabin at the inn, she put the sandwiches together. Four of them. When she asked where he would spend the night, he told her only that he would return in the morning.

With the binoculars and sandwich, he scouted for a suitable watching place. Crouching at the top, he found it: a level area halfway down the face, protected by a shield of upthrust rock.

Before moving down to it, he unwrapped his sandwich, a sourdough roll packed with mayonnaise, jack cheese, and salami. He ate, looking across the distance at the back of Beast House.

The guy was still mowing.

Jud watched through his Bushnell binoculars. The man's hairless head was shiny with perspiration. In spite of the heat, he wore a sweatshirt and gloves. Occasionally he wiped a sleeve across his face.

Poor bastard.

Jud looked down at the sweaty man, appreciating his own comfort: the feel of the breeze on his bare skin, the piny smell of the air, the taste of his sandwich, and the good solid knowledge that he'd found a woman, today, who mattered to him.

Done with the sandwich, he climbed down to the flat area where he'd left his pack and rifle. His shirt was still damp. He loaded it into the pack, along with his binoculars and parka, then returned to his observation point.

## 2.

After the pick-up left the grounds of Beast House, nothing moved inside the perimeter of the fence — nothing within the area visible to Jud, at least. That included the entire back of the house, and its southern side.

Jud wasn't much concerned about the front. In the Thorn and Kutch killings, the assailant had apparently entered by breaking rear windows. He must've come across the yard from the woods behind the house.

If anyone entered tonight, Jud would get a look at him.

But not a shot at him.

That would have to wait. You don't take down a bastard just because he goes into a house at night, or because he's wearing a monkey suit. You've gotta be sure.

He scanned the area with his binoculars. Then he ate another sandwich, washing it down with canteen water.

When the sun was too low to keep him warm, he put on his shirt. It was dry, now, and slightly stiff. He tucked it into his jeans.

Lighting another cigar, he leaned back against the steep rock face. The protective uprise of rocks at the front of his ledge blocked some of his view. The entire backside of the house was still visible, though. He would settle for that. A fair exchange, so he wouldn't have to squat or crouch his way through the night.

After watching the house for an hour, he folded his parka and sat on it. Its thickness not only padded the hard ground but also gave him extra height, improving his view.

As he watched, he thought of many things. He concentrated on what he'd learned of the beast, searching for the most plausible explanation of its identity. Always, he came back to the time element: the first killings in 1903, the most recent in 1977. That certainly seemed to rule out the possibility that one man had performed all the killings.

Yet he couldn't buy the idea that the killer was some ageless, clawed monster. In spite of what Larry had said. In spite of Maggie Kutch's stories.

In spite of the scars on Larry's back?

A human could have made those scars. If not with fingernails, then with the claws of artificial paws. A human dressed up in a monkey suit – or a beast suit.

What about the time element, then? Almost seventy-five years.

Okay, several humans in beast suits.

Okay, who and why?

Suddenly he had a theory. The more he puzzled over his theory, the better it looked. As he began to reflect on ways to gather proof, however, he noticed that darkness had come.

He crawled forward quickly to the stone lip. The house was black. Its lawn was a dark expanse, empty of detail like the surface of a lake on a cloudy night. Reaching into his pack, Jud pulled out a leather case. He opened its snap and removed a Starlight Noctron IV. Putting it to his eye, he made a quick scan of the house and lawn. In the eerie red light generated by his infrared scope, nothing seemed out of place.

When his legs ached from squatting, he backed away from the front. He lowered the Starlight long enough to put on his coat. Then he stood, leaning back against the rock face, and continued his surveillance.

If this theory was correct, he had nothing to gain by spending a cold night up here. He wouldn't see any beast.

Well, it couldn't hurt to stick around.

We should've put somebody inside the house. Bait.

Who'd go in?

Me, that's who.

Too early in the game for that. This is time for surveillance, a good look from a safe distance. Learn the nature of the enemy.

If nothing else, I learn that the enemy didn't enter the house tonight from the rear.

The scope was growing heavy. He put it down and removed the final sandwich from his pack. As he ate it, he watched without the aid of his expensive scope, and could see little except darkness. He finished the sandwich quickly and returned to using the scope.

After a while, he knelt and rested his elbows on the

ledge of the rock. He scanned the yard, the edges of the forest, the gazebo, even the windows of the house, though their glass would block most heat that the scope might pick up.

Leaving the scope in place on the rock, he stepped around his backpack and urinated into the darkness.

He returned to the scope. He swept the grounds. Nothing. He glanced at his wristwatch. Just after ten-thirty. He settled down, then, and watched for nearly an hour without changing position.

During that time, he thought about the beast. Thought about his theory. Thought about other nights he'd spent alone with a Starlight and a rifle. Thought a lot about Donna.

He thought about the way she looked that morning in her corduroys and blouse, hands tucked into the hip pockets of her pants. They became his hands, stroking the warm smooth curves of her rump. Then he saw his hands unfastening the buttons of her blouse, slowly parting it, touching breasts he had never seen but could vividly imagine.

Hard, his penis strained against the front of his pants.

Think about the beast.

Into his mind came the fat, black face of General Field Marshal and Emperor for Life Euphrates D. Kenyata. One of the big, round eyes vanished as a bullet ripped through it and took out the back of the Emperor's skull.

The Beast of Kampala was dead.

And so was Jud's erection.

The guards – if they'd caught him. But they hadn't. They hadn't even come close. No closer than he'd allowed for, at least. Still, if they'd caught him . . .

There!

Just this side of the fence.

He held the scope steady. Though something – probably a bush – blocked portions of the heat mage, he could see that the crouching figure had the basic shape of a human.

It lay down flat. It shoved something forward, apparently through a gap beneath the fence. Then it squirmed under the fence, itself. On the other side, it picked up the object and stood upright on two legs. It looked both ways, turning.

In profile, it had breasts.

It ran to the back of the house, climbed stairs, and disappeared into a porch.

A few seconds passed. Then Jud heard a quick, faint crash of breaking glass.

### 3.

When Jud reached the fence, gasping and hurting from his rush down the dark hillside, he didn't take time to find the burrow. He tossed his flashlight through the bars of the fence, leapt up, and grasped the high crossbar with both hands. He flung himself upward. Stiff-armed, he braced himself above the bar. A muffled scream came from the house. His weight shifted forward too much, and he felt the point of a spike prod his belly. He leaned back, and kicked up his left leg. His foot found the bar. He shoved hard upward, letting go. His right leg cleared the spikes. He fell for a long time. When he hit the ground, he tumbled, rolled to his feet, and retrieved the flashlight. Then he sprinted to the back of the house.

As he rushed up the porch steps, he unholstered his Colt .45 automatic. He wondered briefly if he should change clips – exchange the standard seven-shot magazine for the twenty-shot oversize he kept in his parka. Hell, if he couldn't get it with seven . . . *it?*

Inside the porch, the house door stood open. One of its glass panes was broken.

He entered. He flicked on his flashlight, swung its beam. The kitchen. He ran through a doorway into a narrow hall. Ahead, he saw the stuffed-monkey umbrella holder, and the front door. He shined his light over his left shoulder. It lit the staircase bannister. He rushed to the foot of the stairs, checked to the left and right, then swung his beam up the stairway.

Halfway up, it lit the red of a gasoline can lying on its side. He climbed to the can. Its caps were still in place. A three-foot length of rope had been passed through its handle and knotted, forming a sling. Liquid sloshed inside the can as he set it upright. He holstered his pistol and unscrewed one of the caps. He dropped it into his shirt pocket and sniffed the opening. Gasoline, all right. As he reached into his pocket for the cap, he heard breathing above him. Then a sound of parched laughter.

His beam climbed the stairs, lit a bare leg running blood, a hip, a mauled breast, a face. Hair hung down the face. Blood trickled from its chin. A flap of forehead skin hung down, hiding one eye.

More laughter came, as if trickling from her open mouth along with blood.

'Mary?' Jud called quietly up the stairs. 'Mrs Ziegler?'

She came forward in a strange, gliding way, her arms swinging loosely, her legs barely seeming to move.

Jud lowered his flashlight enough to see that her feet were two inches off the floor.

'Oh God,' he muttered, and started to reach for his pistol.

The body flew down at him.

He dropped to a crouch, bracing hmself. The body struck him, rolled over his back with soft liquid sounds, and fell away. It thudded, hitting the stairs below him.

Then something else hit his back.

He shot his elbow into soft flesh and heard an explosion of breath. Gagging at the sour stench, he drove his elbow backward once more and twisted his body. Something sharp raked his shoulder, tearing his parka and skin as the heavy weight left his back. In pain, he dropped his automatic.

He clawed at the stairs, trying to find it. He found the

gas can instead. He grabbed it. From below came grunting, snarling sounds.

Swinging the can, he splattered gasoline into the darkness. A pale shape appeared, hunched and climbing. He heard gas spatter it. Its arms flailed, and it shrieked. It knocked the can from Jud's hands. He backed up the stairs, reaching into his shirt pocket. Behind the cigar box was a book of matches.

Claws tore his thigh.

He ripped a match free, still climbing backward. He scratched it across the abrasive strip and saw a blue splutter.

The match didn't light.

But the thing was in midair, vaulting the bannister.

It grunted, hitting the floor far below. Then it scampered away towards the kitchen.

Jud searched the stairs until he found his flashlight and gun. Then he sat down, somewhere above the ravaged body of Mary Ziegler, and listened to the house.

# *Chapter Ten*

Roy ached. Especially his shoulders and back. He felt as if he'd been driving forever. Only seven hours, though. He shouldn't feel this bad, not after only seven hours.

He reached into the bag beside him and felt the heat of the Big Macs. He started to pick one up. Then he set it down again. He could wait. He'd be stopping for the night, soon. That would be the time to eat.

As he drove across the Golden Gate, he glanced to the right at Alcatraz. Too dark. He couldn't see much except the signal light. Just as well. What did he want to see a fucking prison for, anyway?

It's not a prison, he reminded himself.

Sure it is. Once a prison, always a prison. It could never be anything else.

If he stayed on 101 another ten minutes, he'd be able to see San Quentin. Shit, as if he hadn't seen enough of that scumhole.

He didn't want to think about it.

He went ahead and took out a Big Mac. He unwrapped it. He ate slowly, watching the freeway signs. As he swallowed the last bite, he flicked on the turn signal and steered the Pontiac Grand Prix up the Mill Valley exit.

Smooth. He liked the way it handled. Bob Mars Bar had good taste in cars.

Mill Valley hadn't changed much. It still had the feel of a small, country town. The Tamalpias Theater marquee was dark. The old bus depot looked the same as always. He wondered if it still had all those paperbacks. Over to the left, the old buildings had been replaced by a huge, wooden structure. The place was changing, but slowly.

A big dog, part Lab, wandered into the intersection. Roy stepped on the gas and swerved to hit it, but the damn thing leapt out of range.

At the end of town, he turned on to a road to Mount Tamalpais, Muir Woods, and Stinson Beach. It meandered into the wooded hills. For a while, he passed scattered, dark houses. Then they were gone. He drove deeper into the woods, sometimes slowing almost to a stop as he took the tight curves.

When he came to a dirt turn-out, he pulled on to it and stopped. He shut off the headlights. Darkness wrapped the car. The dome light came on when he opened the door. He opened the back door and pulled a red Kelty backpack off the seat. After taking a flashlight from one of its side pockets, he shouldered the pack. He shut the car doors and stepped to the edge of the woods.

The ground sloped gradually upward. Bushes caught at his jeans as he climbed. Soon after leaving the road, he tripped over a low strand of barbed wire. A barb punctured his pants, scratching his shin. He jerked his pants leg free and continued upward.

At the top of the slope, he searched through the evergreens. They seemed closely packed. He was about to give up his search when the beam of his flashlight swept through a space that seemed fairly open. He stepped towards it and grinned.

The clearing, about twenty feet around, had a good flat area for his sleeping bag. A circle of rocks remained where someone else had made a campfire. Inside the circle were half a dozen charred cans. Kneeling, Roy touched one of them. Cold.

He scanned the area with his flashlight. All around the clearing, the forest seemed dark and silent.

This would do fine.

He lowered the backpack and opened it. On top was a plastic ground cloth. He spread it out. Then he took out a blue stuff bag, slipped the drawstring loose, and pulled out Bob's mummy bag. He put it on top of the ground cloth.

Should've brought one of those rubber pads, he thought. If only he'd thought of it.

He wandered into the trees, gathering firewood. He picked up handfuls of kindling, and brought them to the circle of rocks. Then he gathered armloads of dead limbs until he had formed a high pile. He tossed the burned cans into the trees.

With toilet paper from the pack, he started the fire. He fed it twigs. It grew, crackling and spitting. Its flames warmed his hands and cast fluttering light through the clearing. He added larger twigs. As the wood caught, he added more.

'Now, there's a healthy fire,' he muttered.

Three good fires in one day. He was getting a lot of practice.

He stood over the fire, watching its flames leap and curl, feeling its heat on the front of his body. Then he stepped back, out of its heat. He picked up the flashlight.

Once in a while, as he worked his way back through the thick woods, he looked over his shoulder. He could see the fire for a long time, its brightness shimmering on leaves over the clearing. By the time he reached the slope overlooking his car, no trace of the fire was visible.

He climbed down slowly, carefully, to the car. From

the front seat, he took the sack from McDonald's. Then he stepped back to the trunk. He unlocked it. The lid swung up.

Joni squinted when the light beam hit her eyes. She was lying on her side, covered by a plaid comforter.

'Hungry?' Roy asked.

'No,' she said in a pouty voice.

The other times he'd opened the trunk, once every hour after leaving Santa Monica, she'd neither spoken nor moved. In fact, she hadn't said a word since last night in the bathroom.

'So, you're not crackers after all.' He pulled the comforter. Joni tried to hold on to it, but couldn't. It jerked out of her hands.

She curled herself more tightly.

'Climb out of there,' Roy said.

'No.'

'Do it, or I'll hurt you.'

'No.'

He reached under her pleated skirt and pinched her thigh. She started to cry. 'What'd I tell you? Now, get out of there.'

On hands and knees, she climbed over the edge of the trunk, and lowered herself to the ground.

Rou shut the trunk. He took the girl's hand. 'We're gonna have a nice camp-out,' he said.

He climbed the slope, pulling Joni behind him. From her struggles and cries, he knew the undergrowth was punishing her bare legs. 'Do you want me to carry you?' he asked.

'No.'

'I'll carry you piggyback, and the bushes won't hurt.'

'I don't want you to. You're bad.'

'I'm not bad.'

'Yes you are. I know what you did.'

'I didn't do anything.'

'You . . .'

'What?'

'You . . .' And suddenly she was making a loud, grating, 'Whaaaaa!' like a baby.

Roy muttered, 'Shit.'

Noisy sobs sometimes interrupted the droning wail, but it would only start again. There was no sign of a let-up. Not until Roy backhanded her cheek. That stopped the bawling. Only stifled sobs remained.

'Sit down,' Roy ordered when they reached the campsite.

Joni dropped to the mummy bag and hugged her knees to her chest. She rocked back and forth on her rump, sniffing.

Roy broke sticks across his knees and built up the fire. When it was high and snapping, he sat down beside Joni. 'This is pretty nice, huh?'

'No.'

'Have you ever been camping before?'

She shook her head.

'Know what I've got in here?' He lifted the white McDonald's sack towards her face. She turned away quickly, but not before Roy saw the craving in her eyes. He sniffed the sack. The aroma of french fries was overwhelming. He reached in, touched the fries, and pulled one out.

'Look what I've got here,' he said.

He held it high, wiggling it like a pale worm. 'It's all yours. Open up.'

She pressed her lips tight and shook her head.

'Suit yourself.' Roy tipped back his head, opened his mouth wide, and dropped it in. It tasted very salty.

He took a can of beer from the pack. The can was dry and warm. He remembered how cold the cans had felt when he took them out of Karen's refrigerator, how they'd left his hands wet. Well, warm beer was better than no beer. When he opened the can, beer sprayed Joni. She flinched, but didn't bother to dry her face. Roy drank, washing the saltiness out of his mouth.

'Have a french fry,' he said, and offered her another

125

one. 'No? Okay.' He ate it. He took the entire bag of fries out of the larger sack. 'There's a Big Mac in here. It's for you.' He chewed the fries, and washed them down. 'I'm not gonna eat it. It's yours.'

'I don't want it.'

'Sure you do.'

'I don't.'

'I bought it for you. You're going to eat it.'

'You're not my father.'

Dangerous territory. He didn't want her bawling again. 'Suit yourself. It's yours, if you want it.'

'Well, I don't. You probably poisoned it.'

'I didn't poison nothing.' He ate more fries, drank more beer. He finished the fries and the beer at the same time. He tossed the oily bag into the fire, and watched the flames take it. Then he got himself another beer. This time he shook the can and aimed it towards Joni, intentionally shooting the spray into her face. She bit her lower lip. Beer dripped from her nose and chin. Roy laughed. 'You should see yourself.'

He took the remaining Big Mac out of the sack and unwrapped it. 'Want it?'

'No.'

He raised it. He opened his mouth wide. Joni's eyes flashed towards it, then away. 'You do want it.'

She shook her head.

'Yes you do. Here.' He held it towards her face. She tightened her lips. 'Open wide.'

Again, she shook her head.

Roy brushed the burger against her closed mouth, leaving a wet trail of juice and dressing. Then he lowered it and waited to see her tongue sneak out.

Her mouth stayed shut.

'Come on, open up.' Again, he rubbed the burger on her closed mouth. 'Do what I say.'

'Mmmm-mmm.'

Roy put down his beer can. He got to his knees.

'Eat, Joni.'

She shook her head.

With his left hand, Roy pinched her nostrils shut and pushed her backward. He held her down tightly against the sleeping bag. For along time, she kept her mouth shut. Finally, with a gasp, she opened up. Roy stuffed in the hamburger: twisting it, breaking it, mashing it into her mouth and chin and nose. When she started to choke, he let go. He flung the remains of the hamburger towards the trees.

Joni sat up, coughing. Her fingers scooped wads of beef and bun out of her mouth.

'Don't get crap on the sleeping bag,' Roy warned. He shoved her forward.

On hands and knees, head close to the fire, she coughed and spit.

Roy watched the rear of her short, pleated skirt, and remembered dressing her that morning. He'd chosen a fresh white blouse, and green skirt. Joni, on the bed, had neither struggled nor cooperated. It had been like dressing a doll. Only different. This doll had real parts, and he'd enjoyed the feel of them. He hadn't put underwear on her. He liked the idea of nakedness under the skirt.

The choking had stopped, but Joni stayed there on her hands and knees, crying.

Roy patted the back of her leg. His touch made her go rigid. He slid his hand up and down, enjoying the curve of the leg and the cool smoothness of the skin. He moved his hand higher. She turned and knocked it away.

Grabbing her arm, Roy pulled her to him. Her mouth was dripping. He wiped it dry with his handkerchief, and threw the handkerchief into the fire.

She hit at his hands as he unbuttoned her blouse. He ignored it. Then she hit his nose. That hurt. He grabbed her hair and twisted it tightly so the pain made her gasp. He kept hold of the hair. She didn't srike him again. When the blouse was off, he let her go. She hugged herself, shivering, while he folded the blouse and set it inside the pack.

'Cold?'

She said nothing.

Roy crawled behind her. He stroked her shoulders and back. He unbuttoned her skirt and lowered its zipper.

'Stand up.'

She shook her head.

Roy pinched her back. 'Stand up.'

She did. Roy pulled the skirt down.

'Keep standing.'

'I'm cold,' she murmured.

'Stand closer to the fire.'

She seemed reluctant to step off the smooth nylon cover of the sleeping bag, but she did. She moved close to the dwindling fire.

'Put more wood on it, if you want.'

He watched her bend down, lift sticks from the pile, and toss them on to the fire. He watched the flames rise. He watched the fluttering orange glow they cast on her skin. He watched her crouch down close to the fire, giving him only a side view of her body.

He unlaced his hiking boots. Pivattas. Bob had good taste in camping gear. He pulled off the boots.

'Stand on the other side,' he said. 'Facing me.'

That's when she ran.

Roy slid up his cuff, pulled his knife. Flipping it, he caught the blade between his thumb and forefinger. He hurled the knife. It whipped end over end, its blade flashing firelight.

The girl almost reached the dark border of the clearing when the knife hit her. Roy heard the thud of its impact. He heard the girl's startled gasp and saw her tumble forward.

Roy took his time pulling on his boots. He didn't bother lacing or tying them. He simply tucked the loose lace ends under the tongues, and got to his feet.

Twigs and pine needles crushed under his soles as he walked towards the sprawled, white body of the girl.

# *Chapter Eleven*

## 1.

A quiet knocking on the door woke Donna. Raising her face from the pillow, she saw that the window was wrong: off to the side instead of directly over the bed. Strange room. Still dark outside. Somebody knocking. Fear made an uneasy flutter in her belly.

Then she recognized the room, and remembered.

Jud. It must be Jud.

She rolled out of bed. Cold. No time, in the darkness, to find her robe. She stepped quickly to the door and opened it a crack.

Larry stood there in striped pyjamas, hugging himself against the chilly wind.

'What is it?' she whispered, alarm knotting her stomach.

'Judge. He's back. He's been hurt.'

She glanced over her shoulder at Sandy's bed, and

decided not to wake the girl. Twisting the handle button, she locked the door. She stepped out, pulled the door shut, and made sure it was secure.

Following Larry across the parking area, she felt the cold breeze and the sway of her breasts inside her nightgown as if she were naked. It didn't matter. Only Jud mattered. Besides, she could borrow something over there to put on.

'How bad is he?' she asked.

'The beast got him.'

'Oh my God!' She remembered the wax figures, shredded and bloody. But he couldn't be like that. Not Jud. He's hurt, but not dead. He'll be fine.

Larry opened the door of Cabin 12. A lamp was on between the beds, but both beds were empty. One had obviously not been slept in. Donna surveyed the room. 'Where is he?'

Larry shut the door and locked it.

'Larry?'

She saw how he looked down her body as if surprised and distracted by the way it showed through the nightgown.

'He isn't here,' Donna said.

'No.'

'If you think you can . . .'

'What?' Larry asked, and looked up from her breasts. His eyes were vague.

'I'm leaving.'

'Wait. Why? I'm sorry if I embarrassed you. I . . . I was just . . .'

'I know what you were just doing. You just thought you'd use Jud as a pretext to lure me over here so you could . . .'

'Oh heavens no. Good heavens.' He laughed nervously. 'Judge asked me to get you.'

'Well, where *is* he?'

'Over here.'

She followed him across the room.

'Judge didn't want to leave blood on the bed, you see.'

He opened the bathroom door. Donna saw a pile of clothes on the floor. Then she saw Jud sitting on the empty tub. Blood sheathed his back and stained the rear of his Jockey shorts. He finished taping a wide bandage on to his thigh.

'That takes care of that,' he said, and looked up at Donna.

She dropped to her knees, leaned over the side of the tub, and kissed him. She pushed a hand through his damp hair.

'You look awful,' she said.

'You should've seen me before I showered.'

'Do you always shower in your shorts?'

'I didn't want to shock you.'

'I see.' She kissed him again, longer this time, taking pleasure in the warm spread of desire through her loins, and wishing Larry would go away.

'I wouldn't spend all night smooching,' Larry said. 'After all, the man *is* bleeding.'

'Would you like to bandage my shoulder?' Jud asked her.

'Sure.'

'Larry's too squeamish.'

'Blood nauseates me,' Larry said, and left the bathroom.

When Donna squeezed a washcloth above the shoulder wounds, water spilled down, rinsing off blood. 'The *beast* did that?'

'Something did,' he told her.

'They look like claw marks.'

'That's how they feel, too.'

She patted them gently with the washcloth.

'Pour on some hydrogen peroxide,' Jud said. 'It's probably by your knees.'

She let it spill over his cuts, fizzing and foaming. Then, with a large gauze pad from the first-aid kit on the toilet lid, she covered the wounds. 'You sure come prepared,' she said, taping the pad in place.

'Mm-hmmm.'

'Any place else need fixing?'

'That should do it. Thank you.'

'Now let's clean you up. Can you keep your leg dry, if we run water?'

'If it isn't too deep.'

She plugged the drain and turned on the water. With his knee up, Jud kept his thigh bandage above the rising water level. Donna shut off the faucets, and began to scrub his back with a soapy washcloth.

'Did you go into the house?' she asked.

He nodded.

'Boy, that's the height of something.'

'You don't approve?'

'You might've been killed.'

'I came fairly close.'

'How did you get away?'

'I threw gas on him. I guess he was afraid he'd go up in flames.'

Jud's back was clean and slick. Leaning over the side of the tub, she kissed it. The skin made her mouth wet. 'All done,' she said.

'Thank you, ma'am. Could you hand me a towel?'

She gave him one, and watched him press it against his upper leg, to keep water from running on to the bandage as he stood.

'I'll be out in a minute,' he said, climbing from the tub.

'Will you?' she asked, smiling at him and trying to look as if she didn't know he was asking her to leave the bathroom.

'Oh, you prefer to stay?'

She nodded. Reaching behind her, she pulled the door shut. Its handle made a snapping sound as she locked it.

'This isn't the most comfortable place in the world,' Jud said.

'It's fine with me.'

Hands brushing her shoulders, Jud slipped the straps of her nightgown down. She let the nightgown fall. The effect on him was immediate. Dropping to one knee, Donna freed the erect penis from his shorts and tugged the shorts down his legs. Then she stood naked in front of him. First, his eyes caressed her. Then his hands traced the curves of her shoulders, the slopes of her breasts. He pulled her against him, the stiff penis prodding her belly.

As they kissed, Donna's hands explored the dips and rises of his back, the firm globes of his buttocks. She moved a hand to the front, and fingered his scrotum, the long smooth shaft of his penis. She felt his fingers down low between her legs, and moaned as they stroked.

Jud kicked the pile of clothes aside. He spread two bathtowels on the floor, and Donna lay back on them, knees high and parted. Jud knelt over her.

She felt the light touch of his tongue, first on one nipple, then on the other. Then came the slippery pushing. He went deep inside her.

Gasping through her open mouth, she tried to stay quiet. Didn't want Larry to hear. But her breath was coming louder now, and she couldn't help the trembling sound of it. Then she no longer cared. There was only Jud on top of her, inside her, filling her, stroking her to an unbearable urgency that tightened and tightened and finally broke. He muffled her outcry with his mouth.

2.

'For heaven's sake, what took you so long?' Larry asked, looking up at them from the television.

'I thought it was rather quick,' Donna said, smiling.

Jud, wearing only a towel and his bandages, took a robe from the room's closet. He put it on and removed the towel.

'So,' Larry said. 'Now that we're both here and you're nicely patched up, would you be good enough to tell us what happened to you?'

'Do you want to stay?' Jud asked Donna.

'I want to know,' she said. 'I'm chilly, though. May I?'

'Help yourself.'

She pulled back the covers of the bed that had not been slept in. She sat on it, propped the pillow against its headboard, and leaned back. 'All set,' she said, and pulled the blankets shoulder high.

Jud told them what had happened: He told of watching the house from the hillside, of seeing the woman enter, of following her inside, of finding the gasoline can on the stairway.

'Ah,' Larry said. 'Good woman. She was going to reduce the filthy place to ashes.'

'I wonder why she waited so long,' said Donna.

'Could be a lot of things. She probably left town after the killings, to bury her husband and boy. Do you know where they're from?' he asked Larry.

'Roseville, out near Sacramento.'

'It'd only take a few days to bury them and get back here. What was she doing the rest of the time?'

'Trying to figure out how to take her revenge, maybe. Then planning for it, making preparations. When I left there tonight, I used a hole under the fence. I think she probably dug that hole, herself. Once her preparations were made, she probably had to work herself up to actually getting in there and doing the job.'

Larry frowned. 'Why, for heaven's sake, did you try to stop her?'

'I didn't go inside to stop her. I went in to find out who she was, and what she was up to. Until I heard the scream.'

'Oh my God.' Donna could feel a chill, in spite of the covers. 'How badly was she hurt?'

'She was dead.'

'The same as the others?' Larry asked.

'The same as the gal in the parlour. Ethel? This one was in fairly much the same shape, if the wax figure was accurate. I gave her a close look, after the . . . killer . . . got away.'

'Could you tell if she'd been sexually molested?' Larry asked.

Jud nodded. 'It was fairly obvious.'

The thought of it made Donna press her legs tightly together. She became aware that she could still feel Jud inside her, as if he had left an imprint. Her fear and repulsion subsided. She wondered, for a moment, how she might arrange to be alone with him again.

'I knew she'd been molested,' said Larry. 'The beast . . . that's its motive. Sexual gratification. Of course, I should be glad, I suppose. That's what saved my life. The creature was more interested in satiating its lust with Tommy . . .'

'I don't think sex is the main thing.'

'Oh?' Larry sounded sceptical.

'Let me give you my theory. I think this beast is a man.'

'Then your theory's shit.'

'Just listen. It's a man in a costume. The costume has claws.'

'No.'

'Listen, damn it. You too, Donna, and see what you think. The original killings, the Thorn lady's sister and kids, were done by Gus Goucher, the man they hanged.'

'No,' Larry said.

'Why not?'

'They were torn apart with claws.'

'According to whom?'

'According to morgue photos?'

'Have you seen those photos?'

'No, but Maggie Kutch has.'

'If you believe her. Who has possession of the photos?'

'Maggie, I suppose.'

135

'Maybe we can get a look at them.'

'I rather doubt it.'

'Okay, we'll let that go for the time being. It's not that important. Gus Goucher's jury must've seen the photos, must've heard testimony . . .'

'According to the old newspaper accounts, they did.'

'And what the jury heard was sufficient for them to condemn the man.'

'Granted.'

'We ought to check this, but I have the impression that, until the Kutch murders thirty years later, Goucher was pretty much accepted as being the Thorn killer.'

'It was made to look like he was. They needed a scapegoat.'

'No. They needed a suspect. He was a likely one. And he was, quite possibly, the guilty one.'

'They hanged Goucher,' Donna said. 'So he certainly wasn't responsible for the attack on Maggie Kutch and her family.'

'In a way, he might have been. Look at what Maggie did after the killings. She moved out of the house, took in Wick Hapson, and opened Beast House for tours. I think she and Wick decided they'd be happier without Mr Kutch, killed him using an MO similar to the Thorn murders, and cooked up this business about a beast to cover themselves. When they saw how much interest there was in this fictional beast of theirs, they decided to profit from it by opening the house for tours.'

Larry shook his head and said nothing.

'One thing,' Donna said. 'I can't see a woman murdering her own children.'

'That part threw me, too. It still throws me, in fact. For their beast story to hold up, though, the kids had to go.'

'She wouldn't do it. No mother could do that.'

'Let's say it's unlikely,' Jud corrected. 'Mothers have been known to murder their own children. What's more likely, though, is that Wick took care of the kids.'

'Your theory is ridiculous,' Larry said.

'Why?'

'*Because there is a beast in that house.*'

'The beast is a rubber suit with claws.'

'No.'

Donna frowned. 'Do you think it was Wick Hapson tonight?'

'If it was Wick, he's damn strong for a man his age.'

'Axel?'

'It can't be Axel. He's too short, too broad in the shoulders, too awkward in his movements.'

'Then who?'

'I don't know.'

'It's the beast,' Larry explained. 'It's not a man in a rubber suit, it's a beast!'

'Just tell us why you're so sure.'

'I know.'

'How?'

'I know. The beast is not human.'

'Will you believe me when I show you its costume?'

Smiling strangely, Larry nodded. 'Of course. You do that. You show me its costume, and I'll believe.'

'How's tomorrow night?'

'Tomorrow night will ...' He was silenced by a knocking on the door.

## 3.

Donna watched Jud cross to the door and open it. 'Well hello,' he said.

'Is my mother here?'

'Sure she is. Come on in.'

Sandy, hair rumpled from sleep and her blue robe a bit too small on her, stepped into the room. When her eyes met Donna's, Sandy sighed with exaggerated relief. 'So there you are. What are you doing in bed?'

'Keeping warm. What are you doing *out* of bed?'

'You were gone.'

'Just for a few minutes.' She looked at Jud. 'I guess I'd better get back now.' She climbed out of bed, and moved with Sandy towards the door. Jud opened it for them. She wanted to kiss him good night, wanted to hold him tightly, feeling his strength and warmth against her body. Not in front of Sandy, though. Not in front of Larry.

'See you in the morning,' she said.

'I'll walk you back.'

'That isn't necessary.'

'Sure it is.'

He walked beside Donna, not touching her. Sandy ran ahead of them. She opened the door and waited.

'You go on in,' Donna told her. 'I'll just be a second.'

'I'll wait.'

'Shut the door, honey.'

The girl obeyed.

Standing against the door, Donna held out her arms to Jud. He stepped close and embraced her. He smelled faintly of soap. 'Cold out here,' she said. 'You're so warm.'

'This morning, you told Larry you're not married.'

'Divorced,' she said. 'How about you?'

'I've never married.'

'Hasn't the right girl come along?' she asked.

'There've been a few "right" ones along the way, I guess. My line of work, though . . . it's too chancy. I didn't want to inflict that kind of life on anyone.'

'What line of work is it?'

'I kill beasts.'

She smiled. 'Is that so?'

'Yep.' He kissed her. 'Good night, now.'

# *Chapter Twelve*

## 1.

A frightened outcry startled Jud awake. He looked through the darkness at Larry. 'You all right?'

'No!' The man sat forward and hugged his knees against his chest. 'No. I'll never be all right. Never!' And he began to cry.

'Once this thing is settled,' Jud said, 'you'll be fine.'

'It'll never be settled. *You* don't even believe there is a beast. A lot of good you are.'

'Whatever it is, I'll kill it.'

'Will you?'

'That's what you're paying me for.'

'Will you cut off its head for me?'

'None of that.'

'I want you to. I want you to cut off its head, and its cock, and . . .'

'Knock that off, will you? I'll kill it. Nothing else.

None of that dismemberment shit. I've seen enough of that.'

'You have?' The voice in the darkness sounded surprised and interested.'

'I did some work in Africa. Saw a lot of heads lopped off. One fellow kept them in his freezer, and liked to shout at them.'

Jud heard quiet laughter from the other bed. The laughter had a strange sound that made him nervous. 'Maybe I ought to take you back to Tiburon tomorrow. I can finish the job alone.'

'Oh no. No you don't.'

'We might both be better off, Larry.'

'I've got to be here when you kill the beast. I've got to see it die.'

## 2.

At six o'clock, Jud's alarm clock woke him up. The alarm didn't seem to disturb Larry. Climbing from bed, Jud stood on the cool floor and removed his leg bandage. The four parallel lacerations were dry, dark marks about three inches in length. They hurt, but they looked as if they would heal without much problem. He went into the bathroom, dropped the blood-sodden bandage on top of his clothes heap, and put a new bandage on his leg. In the mirror, he checked his shoulder bandage. Some blood showed through, but it looked dry. Maybe later he could get Larry or Donna to change it.

He washed up. After he dressed in clean clothes, his suitcase was nearly empty. He tossed its few remaining contents on to the bed, and took the suitcase into the bathroom. There, he piled his torn, bloody clothes into it. He dropped the old bandage in and latched the suitcase. Then he carried it outside.

The morning was quiet, as if nothing were awake yet except a few birds. He glanced at Cabin 9. Donna would be in there, probably asleep. It was a beautiful morning, and he wanted her to be with him. But he wouldn't try to wake her.

He put the suitcase into the trunk of his car and quietly shut the trunk. Then he returned to his cabin. With a washcloth and bar of soap, he carefully scrubbed up every visible trace of blood in the bathroom. The white towels looked okay. So did the other washcloth. The one in his hand was pink with blood.

He peered into the bathroom wastebasket. Its plastic lining held bits of tape and gauze, bandage wrappings, bloody toilet paper. He dropped the dirty washcloth into it and removed the lining.

He carried his first-aid kit and the garbage bag out to his car. Nobody around. He put them in the trunk.

Then, done with the clean-up, he sat on the cabin step and lit a cigar. It tasted fine, the flavour of its smoke blending with the scent of fresh, piny air.

He leaned back, propping his elbows on the stair above him, and grinned. In spite of his wounds, he felt exceptionally fine.

When he was done with the cigar, he drove down Front Street. The town was quiet. He slowed to give a shaggy brown dog time to amble out of his way. A blue-and-white police car was parked in front of Sarah's Diner. The only moving car he saw was a Porsche that approached slowly, as if struggling to stay within a reasonable proximity to the town's thirty-mile-per-hour speed limit.

To his left, Beast House looked barren. To his right, nothing stirred on the property of the house without windows. He slowed when he could see the outcropping of rocks on the hillside behind Beast House. He would have to get up there soon and retrieve his equipment.

But not now.

Beyond town, he made a U-turn and came back. He passed the two houses. On the next block, he parked in front of a closed barber shop. He walked to the Beast House ticket booth.

On its walls, newspaper clippings were framed in glass. Some told of the murders. Others focused on the tours. He read several of the articles. He wanted to read them all, but that would have taken too long. He didn't want to draw too much attention to himself.

He gazed up at the clock face above the ticket window. Then he checked his watch. The first tour wouldn't start for nearly three hours, at ten o'clock.

Stuffing his hands into his front trouser pockets, he strolled farther down the sidewalk. He paused to look at the weathered Victorian house, then started up again, trying his best to look like a tourist with time on his hands and a preference for morning walks.

When he passed the bend, he stepped into the trees and made his way back.

Several yards from the fence, he found an opening that gave him a view of the front of Beast House, but offered good concealment.

Crouching, he began to wait.

## 3.

Just after nine-thirty, a camper van parked on Front Street. A man climbed out, checked the ticket booth, and returned to the van. Out came a woman and three children. Soon a young couple arrived in a VW.

Jud made his way to the road, and walked up to the ticket booth. It was still deserted.

So was the house, unless someone had entered before Jud began his surveillance: nobody had gone in the front while he'd been watching.

As Jud waited near the ticket booth, more people arrived. He watched the windowless house across the street. Its door was shut. The green pick-up truck was still parked in front of the garage.

Finally, ten minutes before the tour was to start, Jud saw Maggie and Wick leave the house. Braced against Wick, she carried her cane but didn't use it. It took them a long time to reach Front Street. They waited for a station wagon to pass, then they crossed.

Wick helped her up the curb, and let go of her arm. She leaned heavily on her cane. 'Welcome to Beast House,' she called out, her voice low but clear. 'My name's Maggie Kutch, and I own it. You may purchase your tickets from my assistant.' She swung her cane towards the ticket booth. Wick was unlocking its door. 'The tickets run four dollars per adult, only two dollars per child under twelve for the experience of a lifetime.'

The people had listened, quiet and motionless. When Maggie stopped talking, those who were not in line already headed for the ticket booth.

Maggie unlocked the turnstile and pushed through it.

"Back for seconds, eh?" Wick asked when Jud reached the ticket window.

'I can't seem to stay away.' He slid a five-dollar bill under the glass.

'Guess your lady friend didn't show up.'

'Who's that?'

'Your lady friend. The gal that cavorted in the street there, showing off her titties.' Wick gave him the ticket and change.

'I wonder where she is,' Jud said.

'More 'n likely in the loony bin.' Wick chuckled, showing his crooked brown teeth.

Jud went through the turnstile. When the entire group was gathered on the walkway, Maggie began to speak.

'I started showing my house to visitors away back in '31, right after the beast struck down my husband and three darling children. You may be asking yourselves why a woman'd want to take people through her house, when it was the scene of such personal tragedy. Well, the answer's easy: m-o-n-e-y.'

A few of the people laughed uneasily.

Maggie limped up the walkway to the foot of the porch stairs. She pointed her cane upward at the balcony. 'Here's where they lynched Gus Goucher.'

Jud listened carefully to the story of Gus Goucher, checking each detail against his theory that the man had, indeed, been guilty. Nothing she said contradicted his view. He followed Maggie up the porch steps. She told of the old door being shot open by Officer Jenson. She pointed out the monkey-paw knocker. Then she unlocked the door and pushed it open.

The pungent odour of gasoline filled Jud's nostrils.

'I must ask your forgiveness for the smell,' Maggie said, entering. 'My son spilled gas yesterday. It won't be so bad, once we're away from the stairs.'

Jud stepped inside.

'You can see how it stained the carpeting there.'

He manoeuvred around others in the group until he had a clear view of the stairway. Nothing. Where Mary's body should have been, there was only a dark stain. All the blood had been nicely scrubbed before someone doused the carpet with gasoline.

# Chapter Thirteen

## 1.

Sunlight on his face woke Roy. He lifted his head off his rolled jeans, and propped himself up with his elbows. The campfire was out. A sparrow, near the campfire remains, was plucking bread from a clump that Joni had probably spit out. The backpack stood upright, closed and safe.

In daylight, the clearing didn't seem nearly as secluded as it had in the dark. The trees surrounding it were farther apart, the spaces between them offering a wider view than he'd thought. Worse, a hillside over-looked the area.

As he looked up at the hillside, he heard an engine. He saw the blue roof of a car rush by.

'Oh shit,' he muttered.

He unzipped the side of the mummy bag and crawled out. Standing, he unrolled his jeans. He reached into them and pulled out his Jockey shorts. Balancing on one foot, then the other, he stepped into them.

He heard voices.

'Oh shit oh shit.'

He sat down quickly on the mummy bag and started pulling on his jeans.

Two hikers, a young couple, came striding along the hillside just above his camp. They wore soft felt hats, like the ones he'd seen in Karen and Bob's closet.

They came closer and closer.

Lifting his rump, he pulled up his jeans. Zipped them. Buckled them.

The couple stepped into the clearing.

He couldn't believe it! The fucking trail ran right past his mummy bag!

'Oh hello,' said the man of the pair. He seemed pleasantly surprised to meet Roy.

'Hi,' said the girl with him. She seemed no older than eighteen.

'Hello,' Roy answered. 'You almost caught me with my pants down.'

The girl grinned. She had a big mouth for smiling, and huge teeth. Also huge breasts. They did a lot of swinging inside her tight, green tank top. She wore white shorts. Her legs looked tanned and powerful.

The man pulled a briar pipe from a pocket of his shorts. 'You camped smack in the middle of the trail,' he said, as if he found it amusing.

'I didn't want to get lost.'

He slipped a leather pouch out of his rear pocket and started filling his pipe. 'What'd you use for water?'

'I did without.'

'There's a public campground about a mile that way.' He pointed his pipe stem at the hill. 'Faucets there, toilets.'

'That's good to know. Maybe I'll head up that way.'

He lit a match and sucked its flame down into his pipe. 'Illegal camping here, you know.'

'I didn't know that.'

'Yep. Anywhere but the public sites.'

'I can't stand those places,' Roy said. 'They're too crowded. I'd rather stay home.'

'They are awful,' agreed the girl.

'Yep,' the man said, and puffed.

'Where are you headed?' Roy asked, hoping to get them on their way.

'Stinson Beach,' said the man.

'How far's that?'

'We plan to get there by noon.'

'Well,' Roy said, 'have a good hike.'

'That's some nice equipment you've got. Where'd you outfit yourself?'

'I'm from L.A.,' he said.

'That so? Been over to Kelty's in Glendale?'

'That's where I bought most of my stuff.'

'I've been there. Bought my boots there, in fact. Back about six years ago.' He looked down fondly at them.

'Who's that in your sleeping bag?' the girl asked.

Roy's stomach clenched. He thought about his knife. It was rolled inside his shirt, within easy reach of his right hand.

'It's my wife,' he said.

The man grinned, gripping the pipe in his teeth. 'You both fit in the same bag?'

'It's cosy that way,' Roy said.

'Do you have room to manoeuvre?' asked the man.

'Enough.'

The man laughed. 'We ought to try that, huh, Jack?'

Jack, the girl, didn't look amused.

'Our bags zip together,' the man. 'You ought to try it that way. Gives a lot more room.'

'What's wrong with her?' Jack asked.

'Nothing, why? 'Cause she doesn't come out? She's a pretty heavy sleeper.'

'Can she breathe in there?' asked the man.

147

'Sure. She always sleeps that way. Far down like that. She doesn't like her head getting cold.'

'Yeah?' The girl named Jack looked sceptical.

'Well, we'd better be off,' said the man.

'Have a nice hike,' Roy told him.

'You too.'

They walked past him. He watched until they disappeared into the trees, then he unrolled his shirt. He raised his pant leg, and slipped the knife into the sheath taped to his calf. Then he put on his shirt.

He took Joni's blouse and skirt out of the pack, and knelt at the head of the mummy bag. He scanned the trees. Nobody around.

Joni groaned as he pulled her out by the arm. She opened one eye, and closed it again. Roy arranged her face-up on top of the bag.

The sight of her sunlit, naked body excited him.

Not now.

Shit, not now.

He pulled the dress up her legs, and fastened it. Then he raised her to a sitting position, and worked the blouse up her arms. He let her fall back. Quickly, he buttoned her blouse.

'Wake up,' he said. He slapped her.

Her eyes squeezed tight at the sudden pain, then fluttered open.

'Get up.'

Slowly, she rolled over and got to her knees. Her hair was bloody and matted to the back of her head where the knife hilt had bludgeoned her.

Breaking camp seemed to take a long time. While he worked, he watched Joni closely. He listened for voices. He kept glancing up the hillside at the trail and the road. Finally, everything was loaded in the pack. He swung it to his shoulders, grabbed Joni's hand, and led her down to the lower road.

A Ford van passed.

He waved and smiled.

When the road was deserted again, he opened the Pontiac's trunk. 'Climb in, honey.'

## 2.

As Roy drove, he heard radio reports about a house fire and double murder in Santa Monica. They didn't give the victims' names, but mentioned a missing eight-year-old girl. He heard nothing about Karen and Bob Marston.

That worried him.

He went over it in his mind: how Karen had spilled the beans about Malcasa Point; how surprised she was when, instead of leaving, he gagged her and really got down to business until she died; how he had waited, hidden in the hall, for Bob to come home; the way Bob shook his head and moaned when he stepped into the bedroom and saw his wife hanging on the door; the sound of Bob's head splitting under the ax; the candle placed carefully in a circle of paper wads, just the way he'd done it at the other place.

Maybe a visitor dropped by and stopped the fire.

Maybe, somehow, the candle blew out.

If the candle blew out, maybe the bodies hadn't been discovered yet.

He couldn't take that chance. He'd better just act as if the car is hot, and get himself a new one.

He swung it on to a dirt turn-out, the tyres flinging up clouds of yellow dust. He got out, opened the hood, and leaned under it, waiting.

Soon he heard the sound of an approaching car. He stayed under the hood and reached towards the fan belt. The car sped past. It kept going. He tried the same tactic with two more cars. Neither stopped.

The next time he heard an engine, he leaned under the hood until the car was close, then stood up and made a frustrated face, and waved. The driver shook his head. His face said, 'Not a chance, buddy.'

Roy yelled, 'Fuck you, too!'

When the next car came, he simply stuck out his thumb. He saw the woman passenger shake her head at the driver. The car kept going. So did the next.

He slammed the hood.

As he stepped to the car's rear, a van approached. A sunburst was painted on its front. The driver was a woman with straight, black hair. She wore a headband, and a leather vest. He saw her right arm point him out. He waved. He liked the looks of her.

But he didn't like the looks of the man who called out the passenger window. 'Car trouble?' The man's voice was raspy. He wore a faded, sweat-stained cowboy hat, sunglasses, and a black, shaggy moustache. His blue Levi's jacket was sleeveless. His upper arm bore the tattoo of a dripping stiletto.

'No trouble,' Roy called. 'I just stopped to take a leak.'

'Power to you.' The man saluted him with a clenched fist, and the van pulled away.

Roy waited until it was out of sight, then opened the trunk. Joni looked up at him. The hot dog he'd bought at Stinson Beach and tossed into the trunk earlier that morning was gone. The can of Pepsi lay open on its side, empty. Must've been tricky, he thought, drinking it in the trunk.

'Climb out,' he said.

He helped her and shut the trunk.

Joni looked around as if wondering where they had stopped, and why. She didn't seem to find the answer. She looked up at Roy.

'We need a new car,' he said. 'You're gonna help us get it.'

He led her along the roadside. When they were fifty or sixty feet from the rear of his car, he told her to lie down in the northbound lane.

Joni shook her head.

Just as well. He really couldn't trust her, anyway. She would probably try to run.

He tried to think of a way to do this without hurting his hand: a rock, a club of wood, or his knife handle would do fine. Maybe too fine. He didn't want to take a chance on killing her. Not yet. So he decided on his hand. Gripping the neck of her blouse, he jerked her forward. As she stumbled towards him, he slammed his right fist against her temple. Her legs went out. He dragged her partway into the road, and set her down. Quickly, he arranged her arms and legs so she looked awkwardly sprawled. Then he returned to his car, ducked into the nearby trees, and waited.

The wait was short.

He grinned, amazed by his good fortune as he watched a black Rolls-Royce round the corner. A man was driving; a woman passenger sat beside him.

The car swerved to miss Joni, then slowed, and pulled behind Roy's Pontiac. The driver stepped out. Leaving the door open, he walked quickly back towards Joni. He was a big man, well over six feet tall, and at least two hundred pounds.

A goddamn football player!

Shit.

The big man knelt beside Joni. He touched her neck, probably trying to find a pulse. The Rolls was about twenty feet from Roy. All the windows were up. The woman, turned away, was looking through the rear window.

The man began to pull off his sports jacket.

Roy lunged from behind the trees. His boots crushed underbrush. The man glanced over his shoulder. The woman began to turn her head. Leaping, Roy's boot thudded on to the hood of the Rolls. The car lurched under his weight. The man was standing. Roy jumped down between the side of the car and the open door. The woman screamed as he thrust himself on to the

151

driver's seat. He pulled the door shut, and locked it a moment before the man arrived.

The screaming woman threw her shoulder towards the passenger door. Roy jerked the neck of her blouse. It ripped, but it stopped her long enough for Roy to grab her hair. He pulled her towards him. Her cheek hit the steering wheel. He forced her head down to his lap, then chopped her neck with the edge of his hand.

The man's face pressed the window, rage in his eyes, fists pounding the glass.

Roy realized that the car was still running. He shifted into reverse and stepped on the gas pedal. The car shot backwards. The big man, staggering after a quick leap aside, looked at him through the tumbling cloud of dust.

He seemed to know.

Roy shifted to drive. As the Rolls sped forward, the man jumped on to the Pontiac's trunk. Roy braced himself. He hit the Pontiac hard. The man's legs flew out. He dropped heavily on to the hood of the Rolls. With a quick shift to reverse, Roy jerked the Rolls backwards and tumbled the man off.

Right off the front.

He sped forward. The car made a satisfying bounce, passing over the man.

Easy as rolling over a log. Roy grinned.

The grin stopped at once.

What if another car comes along?

The woman across his lap was unconscious, maybe dead.

He left the car running, and got out. The man's body lay conveniently close to the rear of the Pontiac. Roy opened its trunk. He didn't want to look closely at the body, much less touch it – not with the way the head had been mashed. But he had no choice. Something made splashy, plopping sounds as he lifted the body. He dropped it into the trunk, and vomited on to it. Then he slammed the trunk shut.

Running back to the girl, he looked down at himself.

His shirts and pants were dripping gore. Though he gagged, he kept running. He lifted Joni, smearing her with the dead man's blood, and carried her to the Rolls. He set her down on the back seat. He ran to the Pontiac, grabbed his backpack, and threw it into the Rolls beside Joni. Then he climbed into the front and swung the car on to the road.

### 3.

Roy drove the Rolls for nearly an hour before he found a side road he liked. It led over bare hills to the left. He was sure it would take him to the ocean, so he turned on to it.

Joni was conscious in the back seat, but so far she had just stayed there, lying on her side, staring forward. The woman in the front seat was dead. Roy didn't like the way her head lay on his lap, but he decided against trying to set her upright: though there was no blood, the struggle for air had left her face hideously contorted. Her skin had a grey-blue tint. If he had her sitting up, people might notice. So he simply accepted the repulsive weight of her head on his lap, just as he accepted the blood on his hands and shirts and pants. He had to accept them, at least until he could find a deserted stretch of shoreline.

This up ahead looked promising.

The road ended a hundred yards from the shore. He parked in the shade. There were no cars in sight. A few cows grazed on the hillside. He got out. Just to the left of the road, the ground slanted down, forming a gorge choked with heavy bushes. A footpath along the edge of the gorge led to a beach.

He would like to get the woman's body into the water, tow it far out, and let it go. But carrying it to the water would be tough. Dangerous, too. Forget it.

He would roll her into the gorge.

Not now, though. Not until he and Joni were cleaned

153

up and ready to leave. In the meantime, he couldn't just leave her in the front seat. Someone might come along.

He thought of the trunk.

Then he got a better idea. Checking once again to be certain he was unobserved, he got out and pulled her across the front seat. Her feet hit the road, knocking off one of her platform shoes. He dragged her in front of the car. There, he stretched her out lengthwise on the dirt shoulder. Her arms and legs were a little stiff, but he managed to straighten them. With her legs together and her arms flat against her sides, Roy went back to the car.

He drove slowly forward.

Over the top of the black hood, he watched as the car seemed to swallow her.

He stopped and climbed out. He had to get down on his hands and knees to see her in the darkness beneath the car.

A great hiding place.

He pulled Joni out of the back seat. Together, they walked down the footpath to the beach.

## 4.

The water, cold at first, quickly lost the shock of its chill and felt almost warm to Roy. Joni still stood on the shore. Only the largest waves reached far enough to wash over her feet.

Roy took off his shirt. He scrubbed the cloth with his knuckles, trying to wash it. Waves caught him, lifted him, turned him. When they carried him too far from Joni, he swam closer. He held up his blue shirt and studied it in the sunlight. If blood remained on it, which he didn't doubt, at least the stains were barely noticeable.

'Come on in, Joni, and wash up.'

She shook her head. She stepped backwards, farther from the water, and sat down on the sand.

'You know what happens,' Roy called, 'when you don't do like I say.'

She looked down the beach, where a point of rocks jutted into the water. Breakers smashed against the rocks, splashing white froth high. She looked up in the beach. In that direction, the shoreline curved inward and disappeared. 'Don't try it,' Roy yelled, wading forwards.

She stood up and walked into the water. It wound around her ankles. She kept moving. A high wave came, wetting her to the waist, sticking the pleated skirt to her skin. She stopped there. The water receded. Bending, she splashed it on to the bloodstains on her blouse. She rubbed the stains. A wave came, knocking her backwards. She fell, and the white water swirled over her head.

Roy went to her. He lifted her. He kissed her forehead. Then, wrapping his hand in his shirt, he scrubbed the bloodstains on her blouse. They grew faint, but wouldn't vanish altogether. Finally he gave up.

He pulled her deeper into the water, and did his best to wash the blood from her hair. Whenever he touched the sensitive wound left by the knife's hilt, she jerked her head away. Finally her hair was clean enough to suit him. He led her out of the water.

On the beach, he removed her blouse and skirt. He spread them on the sand to dry. Then he took off his own clothes, and spread them next to hers.

They sat down on the sand. It was hot under Roy, almost burning.

'Try to sleep,' he said.

Joni lay back and shut her eyes.

Roy looked at her. Water made tiny points of her eyelashes. Her skin was lightly tanned, except where a two-piece bathing suit had left it pale. Just like a little lady.

155

Beads of water rolled down her skin, glinting sunlight. He wished he had oil. Suntan oil, or baby oil. He would rub her all over with it. Her skin would be slick and hot.

He lay on his side, and propped himself up on an elbow to look at her. Her eyelids fluttered. She was only pretending to sleep, of course.

She opened her eyes when he touched her.

She turned her head and stared at him. He wondered, briefly, if she looked so sad because of what happened to her parents, or because of what he'd been doing to her.

Not that he gave a shit.

Inching closer, he kissed her on the mouth. His hand began moving down her sun-hot skin.

# Chapter Fourteen

## 1.

'We oughtta be getting it in today, lady. That's all I can tell you. When we get it in, I'll install it.'

'Do you think the car will be ready today?' Donna asked.

'Like I say, depends when the radiator gets here.'

'How late are you open?' she asked.

'Till nine.'

'Can I pick up my car, then?'

'If it's done. Stu'll let you take it. I go off at five, though. Stu's no mechanic. If it doesn't get done by five, it doesn't get done till tomorrow.'

'Thank you.'

She found Sandy nearby, eyeing a vending machine. 'Can I get some potato chips?' the girl asked.

'Well . . .'

'Please? I'm starving.'

'We'll eat pretty soon. Why don't you wait, and have potato chips with your meal?'

'Where can we eat around here?' she asked, leaving the machine behind.

'I'm not sure,' Donna admitted.

'Not that place we went yesterday. It was so gross.'

'Let's try this way.' They started walking south on Front Street.

'When's the car gonna be ready?'

'Who knows?'

'Huh?' Sandy wrinkled her nose. When she unwrinkled it, her huge sunglasses slipped forward. She shoved them into place with a forefinger.

'The guy at the station wasn't up to telling me when it'll be ready. But I have a feeling we'll still be here tomorrow.'

'If Dad doesn't get us first.'

The mention of him jolted Donna. Somehow, after meeting Jud, fears of her ex-husband had been pushed into a dark corner of her mind and forgotten. 'He doesn't know where we are.'

'Aunt Karen does.'

'Tell you what, let's give Aunt Karen a call.' Looking around, she saw a phone booth at the corner of the Chevron station they had just left. They backtracked to it. 'How much are the potato chips?'

'Thirty-five cents.'

She handed Sandy a dollar bill. 'You'll have to get change from the man.'

'You want anything?'

'No thanks. But you go ahead.'

She watched her daughter leave, then she stepped into the telephone booth. Her coins rang inside the machine. She dialled Operator, and asked for the call to be charged to her home phone. When the call went through, she heard the ringing of her sister's phone. It was picked up after the second ring. Donna waited for Karen's voice. She heard only silence.

'Hello?' she finally said.

'So.'

'Bob?' she asked, though the voice didn't sound much like his. 'Bob, is that you?'

'Who is this, please?'

'Who is *this?*'

'Sergeant Morris Woo, Santa Monica Police Department.'

'Oh my God.'

'So. Your business, please, with Mrs Marston?'

'I was just ... she's my sister. Has something happened to her?'

'Where are you calling from, please?'

How do I know you're a cop? she asked herself. And she answered, I don't. 'I'm calling from Tucson,' she told him.

'So.'

In her mind, she saw him hang up and turn to Roy, grinning that he'd obtained the information so easily. But he didn't hang up.'

'Please, what is your name?'

'Donna Hayes.'

'So. Address and telephone number?'

'What's happened to Karen?'

'Please. Does your sister have relatives in the Los Angeles area?'

'Damn it!'

'So. Mrs Hayes, I regret your sister met with death.'

*Met with death?*

'She and her husband, Robert Marston, met with death yesterday night. So. If there are relatives ...'

'Our parents.' She was numb. 'John and Irene Blix.'

'Blix. So, Mrs Hayes, may I have please their address?'

She told him their address and phone number.

'So.'

'They were ... murdered?'

'Murdered, yes.'

159

'I think I know who did it.'

'So?'

'What do you mean, *so?* Damn it, I know who killed them!'

'So. You tell me, please.'

'It was my ex-husband. His name is Roy Hayes. He was released yesterday – I mean Saturday. Sometime Saturday.'

'So. Released from what?'

'San Quentin.'

'So.'

'He was in six years for raping our daughter.'

'So.'

'So he must've killed Karen to find out where I am.'

'Did she know, please?'

'Yes, she knew.'

'So. You are in danger. Describe your Roy Hayes, please.'

As she gave the man a description of her ex-husband, she saw Sandy returning with a bag of potato chips. The bag was open. Sandy was pinching chips, one at a time, and pushing them sideways into her mouth.

'So. He drives?'

'Yes, but I don't know what. He may have taken one of Karen's cars. They've got a yellow Volkswagen and a white Pontiac Grand Prix.'

'So. The years?'

'I don't know. She looked at her daughter munching potato chips outside the booth. Turning away, Donna began to cry.

'Please, Mrs Hayes. Are the cars new?'

'The VW, it's a '77. I don't know about the other. A '72, '73.'

'So. Very good, Mrs Hayes. Very good. Now, if I may suggest, call the Tucson police, so, and inform them of your situation. Perhaps an escort to the airport.'

'Airport?'

'So. Your parents are not to be alone during this time of tragedy.'

'No. You're right. I'll get there as soon as I can.'

'So.'

'Thank you, Mr Woo.' She hung up. Sandy knocked on the plastic wall of the booth. Ignoring her, Donna searched her purse for coins. She found them, and made another call.

'Santa Monica Police Department,' said a woman. 'Officer Bleary speaking. May I help you?'

'Do you have a Morris Woo?'

'Just a moment, please.'

Donna heard a telephone ring. It was picked up. 'Homicide,' said the man. 'Detective Harris.'

'Do you have a Morris Woo?'

'He's not in just now. May *I* help you?'

'I talked to a man on the phone.' She sniffed, and rubbed her nose. 'He claimed to be a Sergeant Morris Woo. I just wanted to make sure he's really a police officer.'

'So?'

## 2.

After a brief, tearful call to give her parents the news, she hung up and left the booth. 'Let's go back to the motel.'

'What's wrong?' Sandy was crying. 'Tell me!'

'Aunt Karen and Uncle Bob. They've been killed.'

'No they haven't!'

'I just talked to a police officer, honey.'

'No!'

'Come on, let's go back to the motel.'

Instead, the girl threw herself against Donna, hugging tightly as she cried.

# Chapter Fifteen

## 1.

When Jud climbed out of his car, he saw Donna sitting on a front step of her cabin and he knew that something was wrong. He went towards her. She saw him, and stood. He took her in his arms, and she began to cry softly, quietly, her back trembling under his hand. Jud stroked the back of her head. Her cheek was wet against his face. He held her for a long time.

Then Donna looked up at him. She sniffed, smiled an apology, and rubbed her face with her sleeves. 'Thanks,' she said.

'Are you okay?'

She nodded, her lips pressed tightly shut. 'Can we go for a walk?' she asked.

'I know a nice place. We'll have to go in the car, though.'

'Before we go, I'd better get registered for tonight.'

'Good idea,' Jud said. 'I'll have to do that, too.'

Together, they went to the motel office. They registered. They then returned to Jud's car. 'Where's Sandy?' he asked.

'Sleeping.'

'She seems to do a lot of that, doesn't she?'

'It's a good way to escape.'

'Is she all right?'

'No. Probably not.'

They climbed into the Chrysler, and Jud drove out to Front Street.

'We saw your car in town this morning,' Donna said in an obvious attempt to change the subject.'

'I took the tour again.'

'You mean they *had* a tour? I would've thought the police . . .'

'The police don't know about the killing, apparently. The body's gone. So's the blood. It looks like somebody did a nice clean-up job.'

'Scrub-a-dub-dub.' Donna met his glance, and frowned. 'That's what Axel does. He's in charge of cleaning the place.'

'Axel's in this thing up to the armpits. So's his mother. They all are. It's a family enterprise. All it takes is a murder, now and again, to keep the tourists coming.'

'If the body's gone, though . . .'

'I think they got nervous, killing someone so close to the other three. Nervous enough to pretend it didn't happen.'

'Why did they kill her – they? Now you've got me believing it. Why did they kill her, if they didn't want the publicity?'

'She was gonna burn the place down.'

'I guess that's a good enough reason. What's your next step? Do you try to find her body?'

'That wouldn't do us much good. What we've gotta find is the man in the monkey suit.'

'Then what?'

'If I have to, I'll kill him.'

'You *intend* to kill him, don't you?'

'I doubt if he'll give me a choice.'

They were silent as they drove past Beast House. After they rounded the bend, Donna said, 'Have you killed very many people?'

'Yes.'

'Do you . . . think about it much?'

He glanced at her, then steered on to the shoulder of the road and stopped. 'You mean, does my conscience bother me?'

'I guess that's what I mean.'

'I never killed a guy who didn't have it coming.'

'Who judges that?'

'Me. I judge him and sentence him.'

'How can you?'

'I hear voices.'

She smiled. 'I'm serious.'

'So am I. I hear a voice. It's usually mine saying, I'd better nail this bastard before he nails me.'

'You're awful.'

He laughed softly. And then he felt a cold tightness inside him. He swallowed. 'Sometimes what I hear are the voices of the dead. People I never knew. People I saw in news photos, or with my own eyes. They say to me, "I'd be alive today if this bastard hadn't cancelled my ticket." Then I look at the living and they say, "That bastard's gonna kill me tomorrow." And then I judge him and then I execute him if I can. I figure I'm paying him back for the dead, and I'm saving a few lives. Maybe this sounds terrible, by my conscience is pretty happy with itself.'

'Do you kill for money?'

'If he's the kind of guy I'm willing to kill, there's always someone who's glad to pay me for it.'

They got out of the car. Jud took Donna's hand and led her across the road. 'Do you mind a work-out?'

'Okay by me.'

They entered the forest. Jud went first, seeking out ways through the tightly grouped pines and around impassable areas of rock or fallen trees. Twice, he stopped to let Donna rest.

'You didn't tell me this was an obstacle course,' she said at one point.

The last few yards were steep, and Jud looked back at Donna. Her face was determined. She backhanded a drop of sweat off the end of her nose. Wet hair clung to her forehead. 'Almost there,' he said, and reached down a hand to her. He pulled her to the top of a dead trunk, then they both hopped down. 'Made it.'

They walked easily along the level crest of the hill and came to a windy clearing.

Donna stretched, spreading her arms. 'Ah, that breeze feels good.'

'You can wait here. I've got to pick up a few things down below.'

'So that's your game!'

She accompanied Jud to the edge of the clearing, when he pointed down to the outcropping. 'I left some equipment in those rocks, he told her.

'That's where you were last night?'

'That's the place.'

'I'll go with you, okay?'

Together, they climbed downhill. Then they made their way up the rocks to the top, where they looked down at the back of Beast House.

'I can't imagine going in that place at night,' Donna said. 'It's bad enough in daylight.'

'I'll climb down and get my gear,' Jud said.

'Fine. I'll wait.'

As Donna sat on a ledge of rock, Jud worked his way down to the recess with its two small pines. His pack and rifle and Starlight seemed just as he had left them last night when he rushed downhill to stop the woman. He put the scope in its case and loaded it into the pack. He strapped the pack shut. Then he slung it on to his shoulders. He picked up the rifle case and climbed to the top.

'Let's go up to the clearing again,' Donna said.

'Sure.'

'I don't much like staring that house in the face.'

'That's actually the back of its head,' Jud told her.

'Whatever.'

They climbed to the grassy clearing. Jud put down his rifle and pack. Donna, stepping close, placed her open hands against his chest and looked up at him. 'Can we talk some more?' she asked.

'Sure.'

'About killing?'

'If you want.'

'What happened today . . .' She lowered her eyes. 'What happened was, I found out my . . . sister . . .' Her voice broke. She turned away. With her back turned, she took a deep breath. Jud put his hands on her shoulders. 'My sister was killed!' she blurted, and broke into tears.

Jud turned her around and held her tightly.

'I *killed* her, Jud. I killed her. I ran away. He wouldn't have done it. He wouldn't have had to. God! I didn't know. I didn't *know!* I killed them. I killed them both!'

## 2.

After a while, Donna settled down. She stopped talking, and only cried. Jud lowered her to the grass. Sitting against his pack, he held her. Her tears made the front of his shirt wet. Finally she stopped.

'We'd better get back,' she said. 'Sandy. I don't want to leave her alone too long.'

'We'll leave when you tell me what's going on. Who killed your sister, Donna?'

'My ex-husband, Roy Hayes.'

'Why?'

'Partly to get at me, I guess. Mostly, though, to make her tell where I am.'

'Why would he want to know that?'

'He's been in prison. He . . . raped Sandy. She was just six, and he took her out riding on his dirt bike . . . and raped her. He'd done things to me, before. Vicious things.

'I knew they'd let him out, someday. I figured we'd drop everything, and take off. So that's what we did Sunday morning when I found out he was loose.

'It never . . . it just didn't occur to me he'd go to Karen. I don't know what I thought. But I never . . . God, I never thought he'd go to Karen or anyone, and . . . he must've tortured her. God, and it was all because of me!

'We shouldn't have run. We should have stayed. I should have got myself a gun, maybe, and just waited for him to come. But it never even occurred to me. I just thought we'd leave town, and maybe change our name, and everything would work out fine. But it didn't happen that way. And now he knows where we are.'

'Where did your sister live?'

'In Santa Monica.'

'What's that, ten or twelve hours from here?'

'I don't know. Something like that, probably.'

'Do you know when your sister was killed?'

'Sometime last night.'

'Early, late?'

'I don't know.'

'He could be in town right now.'

'I guess so.'

'What does he look like?'

'He's thirty-five, about six-foot-two. Very strong, or he always used to be. He weighed about two-ten.'

'Have you got a picture of him?'

She shook her head. 'I destroyed them all.'

'What colour's his hair?'

'Black. He always wore it short.'

'Anything else about him?'

She shrugged.

Jud got up and helped her to stand. 'Are you convinced,' he asked, 'that running away doesn't work?'

'He convinced me.'

'Then let's go back to the inn and wait for him.'

'What'll we do?'

'If I have to, I'll kill him.'

'I should be the one to handle him.'

'Not a chance. You're stuck with me.'

'I don't want you to kill anyone . . . not for me.'

'I wouldn't be doing it for you. It'd be for myself. And for the voices.'

# Chapter Sixteen

## 1.

'Larry and I have to go out for a while,' Jud said as he walked Donna across the parking lot after lunch. 'I want you and Sandy to stay in our cabin until we get back.'

'Okay.'

No arguments. No questions. Her complete trust gave Jud a good feeling.

He watched her turn to Sandy, who was lagging behind with Larry. Instead of making a rift, yesterday's incident at the beach had created an intimacy between the girl and Larry. During lunch, they had talked like best friends. Jud found their closeness peculiar under the circumstances, but convenient.

'Sandy,' Donna said, 'we'll be spending a while in Jud and Larry's room. Do you want to get your cards, or a book, or something to keep you busy?'

The girl nodded.

'We'll be right out,' Donna said. They went into their cabin, leaving its door open.

Larry, in a quiet voice, said, 'The poor child has been devastated.'

'It's gonna be rough.'

'Rough indeed. She'll be scarred all her life. That miserable brute ought to be shot.'

'He probably will be.'

'I certainly hope so.'

'Tonight, if we're lucky.'

'Tonight?'

'There's a good chance he'll show up sometime today. If he does, I'm going to be there with a gun.'

'What about Beast House?'

'It can wait another day.'

'I suppose you're right, though I *would* feel better if we were finished once and for all with . . .'

'I can't let this guy get his hands on Donna and Sandy. He's hurt them enough, already.'

'Certainly. I'm not suggesting we abandon them. Not at all.'

'Besides, going after the beast tonight would be premature.'

'How so?' Larry asked.

'I want to know more. That's why we're going to visit the Kutch place this afternoon.'

'Beast House?'

'No. The other one. The one without windows.'


2.


As soon as Jud was certain that Donna could handle his rifle without difficulty, he and Larry drove away. He turned right off Front Street, taking the narrow dirt road that led to the beach. In an area sheltered by trees, he parked.

As Jud took his .45 automatic from the trunk, Larry said, 'That, of course, won't stop the beast.'

Jud tucked the automatic under the belt at the back of his pants, and covered it with his shirt tail. 'What makes you think we'll run into the beast? Doesn't it confine its rampages to Beast House?'

'Nevertheless.'

He watched Larry lift a machete out of the trunk. 'Nevertheless what?'

'One never knows, does one?'

Jud shut the trunk. 'You can stay in the car, if you want.'

'No. It's quite all right. I'll come along. I can hardly resist an opportunity to see inside this curious house. And you're right, of course: we should be perfectly safe from the beast.'

Jud checked his wristwatch. 'Okay, the one-o'clock tour should just be staring. Let's go.'

'What about Axel?'

'If he's home, I'll take care of him. You just stick close beside me.'

'I certainly hope you know what you're doing.'

Jud didn't answer that. He led the way through the trees until they ended. Then he dashed across an open space to the back of the garage. Larry followed.

'Do you know if there's a back door?'

'I'm not certain.'

'Let's find out.' He walked towards the rear, careful to keep the garage between him and the ticket booth of Beast House, a hundred yards away. When he was even with the rear of the brick house, he rushed across to it.

The back of the house was solid brick.

'No door,' Larry said.

Jud walked through the overgrown yard to the far corner. He peered around it. No door there, either: just the grey metal box of the house's ventilation system. Across Front Street, the south part of Beast House's fence and lawn were visible, and deserted. 'Stay close to

173

the wall,' Jud said. He wiped sweat off his brow and moved forward.

At the front corner of the house, he stopped. Signalling Larry to stay back, he looked at the ticket booth across the street. The side that faced the street had a closed door, but no windows. As long as Wick Hapson stayed inside, he wouldn't be able to see Jud.

Beyond the ticket booth, the tour group was clustered near the Beast House porch, probably hearing about Gus Goucher. Jud waited for them to file inside.

'Stay here till I signal.'

'Is Axel home?'

'His pick-up's here.'

'Oh dear.'

'That's all right. It might make things easier.'

'For heaven's sake, how?'

'If he's a trusting soul, the door won't be locked.'

'Wonderful. Marvellous.'

'Wait here.' Jud again checked the ticket booth, then walked swiftly across the front lawn to the door.

The inner door stood wide open. Jud pressed his face to the screen door, trying to see inside. He couldn't see much. Except for the light from the doorway, the interior was dark. Quietly, he pulled open the screen door, and entered.

He moved quickly away from the lighted area. For at least a full minute, he stood motionless, listening. Convinced he was alone, he patted the walls near the door and found a switch. He flicked it. A lamp came on, its bulb filling the entryway with dim, blue light.

Directly ahead, stairs led to the upper floor. To the right was a closed door, to the left a room. He stepped into the room. By the faint light from the foyer, he found a lamp. He turned it on. More blue bulbs.

Dark carpeting covered the floor. Pillows and cushions littered it. A lamp stood in a back corner. There was no other furniture.

Jud went to the screen door. Looking through it, he

checked the area near the ticket booth for Wick Hapson. No sign of the man. He opened the door a crack and waved to Larry.

Before Larry reached the door, Jud pressed a forefinger to his own lips. Larry nodded and entered.

Jud pointed out the room with the cushions. Then he stepped to the closed door at the right of the entrance. He pushed it open and found a light switch. It turned on a chandelier over a dining-room table. The chandelier bulbs were blue.

Except for the lighting, Jud found nothing unusual about the dining room. A china cabinet stood in one corner. A large mirror occupied the far wall above a buffet. The table had six chairs, but formal dining tables often had that many. He saw two more matching chairs beside the highboy.

Beyond the head of the table was another door. Jud went to it and pushed it open. The kitchen. He entered it, careful to walk quietly on the linoleum floor. He looked in the refrigerator. Even its interior light was blue. Pointing at the botom shelf, he grinned at Larry. The shelf held at least two dozen cans of beer.

Next to the refrigerator was a door.

As he began to pull it open, Jud saw light on the other side. Blue light. He opened it farther and looked down a steep flight of stairs to the cellar.

He shut it quietly. Stepping around Larry, he went to the dining room. He brought one of the straight-backed chairs into the kitchen and tipped it against the door, bracing its back under the knob.

Then he motioned for Larry to follow.

They went from the kitchen to the foyer and silently climbed the stairs. Just off the hallway at the top was a large bedroom. They entered it, and Jud turned on its blue overhead light. Larry flinched, and slapped the hilt of his machete. Then he laughed quietly, nervously, 'How exotic,' he whispered.

Mirrors ran the length of the walls, and one was

attached to the ceiling directly above the large bed. There were no blankets on the bed, only blue satin sheets.

As Larry knelt to look under the bed, Jud checked the closet. The hangers held nothing except robes and more than a dozen nightgowns. He pulled out one of the nightgowns and it filled with air, swaying as if it had no weight at all. Dainty pink bows at the shoulders and hips were all that connected the front and back of the gown. Through the sheer fabric, Jud could see Larry stepping over to the bureau. Jud put the nightgown away.

'Oh dear!' Larry muttered.

Jud rushed over to Larry. The open drawer held four pair of handcuffs. Looking in another drawer, he and Larry found a pile of steel chain with padlocks. In another was an assortment of bras and panties, garter belts, and nylons. Two of the drawers contained only leather: leather slacks and jackets, brief leather bikinis, vests, and gloves. From a hook at the side of the dresser hung a riding crop.

They shut all the drawers and left.

The bathroom smelled of disinfectant. They quickly searched it, finding nothing unusual except for the sunken bathtub. It was large, perhaps seven feet by four, with several metal rings fixed into the tile walls at head level.

'What are those for?' Larry asked.

Jud shrugged. 'They look like handles.'

At the far end of the hall, they entered a small room with bookshelves, a desk, and a stuffed chair. By the blue overhead light, Jud made his way to a lamp behind the chair. He turned it on.

'Ah, light,' Larry whispered as white light filled the room. He began to inspect the book titles.

Jud checked the desktop, then the drawers. The drawer on the upper left was locked. Kneeling, he removed a leather case from his pocket. He took out a pick and tension bar, and worked on the lock. It gave him no trouble at all.

The drawer was empty except for a single leather-bound book. A strap with a lock held it shut like a diary. He quickly picked that lock and opened the book to its title page. 'My Diary: Being a True Account of My Life and Most Private Affairs, Volume 12, in the year of our Lord 1903.' The name beneath the inscription was Elizabeth Mason Thorn.

'What do you have there?' Larry asked.

'The diary of Lilly Thorn.'

'Good heavens!'

He thumbed through the pages. Three quarters of the way through, he found the final entry. August 2, 1903. 'Last night, I waited until Ethel and the boys were asleep. Then I carried a length of rope down cellar.' He shut the diary. 'We'll take it,' he whispered. 'Now let's have a look in the other room and get out of here.'

The door of the room across the hallway was shut. Jud twisted the knob. He inched it open.

Larry clutched his arm.

From inside the room came a strange, windy sound. Jud listened closely, ear to the crack. He heard hisses, sighs, a blowing sound like the wind makes coming down a canyon. He silently closed the door.

When they got downstairs, Larry whispered, 'That was the beast. It was in there sleeping.'

'I think it was just Axel.'

'Axel, my foot!'

'But he wasn't alone,' Jud said.

'Indeed not!'

'I heard at least three people in that room. Let's get out of here.'

'Marvellous suggestion. I'm with you 100 per cent.'

# Chapter Seventeen

The green, metal sign read, 'WELCOME TO MAL-CASA POINT, pop. 400. Drive with care.' Roy slowed down to 35 miles per hour.

He saw a dozen people lingering near a ticket booth in front of an old Victorian house. He glanced at the sign. Its red lettering wobbled and dripped like wet blood. BEAST HOUSE. He grinned, and wondered what the hell it was.

Slowing, he studied the faces of the people near the ticket booth. None looked at all like Donna or Sandy, not even with the changes six years might bring. He kept moving.

He watched the sidewalks for them; he watched the road and parking spaces for their car. A blue Ford Maverick, Karen had said. She wasn't lying. At that point, she had been beyond lying.

When he saw a blue Maverick parked at a Chevron station, he couldn't believe his luck. Karen had mentioned car trouble, but that shouldn't take so long to repair: he'd expected Donna to have a day on him, at least.

He stopped beside a row of gas pumps. A skinny, sneering man approached his window. 'Fill 'er up with Supreme,' Roy said, and wondered if Supreme was what the Rolls took. He decided the gas jockey would've made a remark if it didn't. The guy'd said nothing.

Roy climbed out. It felt good to stand and stretch. His jeans were still damp in the pockets. He scratched his itchy skin and stepped to the rear of the car.

'That Maverick over there,' he said. 'It wouldn't belong to a woman travelling with her daughter, would it?'

'Might.'

'The woman's thirty-three, blond, a real fox. The kid's twelve.'

The guy shrugged.

Roy pulled a ten-dollar bill from his wallet. The man eyed it for a moment, then took it and stuffed it into his shirt pocket.

'What's the woman's name?' Roy asked.

'I can check.'

'Is it Hayes? Donna Hayes?'

He nodded. 'That's her. I remember the Donna.'

'And she had a kid with her?'

'Little blond gal.'

'How long you been working on the car?'

'Couple days. We brought her in Monday morning. That's yesterday. Busted radiator. We had to send over to Santa Rosa for a new one, just got it in.'

'So they're staying in town?'

'I don't know where else they'd be.'

'Where are they?'

'Only one motel. That's the Welcome Inn, about a half mile up the road, on your right.'

Roy gave the man another five dollars. 'That's to keep your mouth shut.'

'How come you're looking for her?'

'I'm her husband.'

'Oh yeah?' He laughed. 'She run out on you?'

'That's right. And I'm aiming to fix her for that.'

'Don't blame you a bit. She's a choice piece, that gal. I'd be pissing steam if she run out on me.'

Roy paid for the gas, then drove half a mile up the road. He saw the restaurant first, a rustic building shaded by evergreens. 'Welcome Inn's Carriage House. Fine Dining.' A short distance beyond it was a coffee shop. Then a driveway led into a courtyard with about half a dozen cabins on each side. Just past the driveway entrance stood the motel office. The red tubing of the neon 'Vacancy' sign was lit.

Roy kept driving, suddenly nervous.

So close. He didn't want to blow it, now. He needed time to think.

He drove up the road until he found a wide shoulder. There, he pulled off and shut down the engine. He checked his wristwatch. Nearly three-fifteen.

Donna's car is at the Chevron station, he thought. Okay. If she picks it up today, she either leaves right away, or spends the night. If she leaves, she'll drive past here. He could simply wait and stop her somehow.

What if she heads south? No, she wouldn't do that. Not after making a beeline north like this.

Still, she might.

Or she might stay another night at the Inn.

That'd be easy enough to find out. Just check in the motel office. If she's planning to stay over, she would've registered by now.

He couldn't check the office, though. She might find out.

Well, not necessarily. He could go to the office, get her cabin number, and drive right to her door before she had a chance to find out anything, take precautions, call the cops. He could bust in, grab her and the kid, get out before anyone knows what hit.

Not a chance. People would see. There'd be cops after them so quick. . . .

Why take them anywhere? Just go in, shut them up, and stay inside. Plenty of privacy. Even beds. Stay as long as he felt like it.

What if they're out?

If they're out, they might ask at the office, and find out he'd been there asking.

'Shit,' he muttered, seeing his plan fall apart.

Okay, getting the number from the office is out. That leaves one way to learn which cabin is theirs: stake the place out. Watch for them.

He spent a few moments wondering about the best way to keep watch on the cabins, then climbed out of the car. He took his pack from the back seat and slipped his arms through the straps. Then he opened the trunk. Joni was conscious. He lifted her out by the arms.

They walked along the roadside until Roy saw the office of the Welcome Inn about fifty yards ahead. Then he led Joni into the trees. The twigs and pine cones of the forest floor hurt her bare feet, and she started to cry.

'Stop that.'

'It hurts.'

'Do you want me to carry you?'

She nodded.

Roy grinned, remembering how she'd refused a similar offer, just last night. Maybe she was beginning to trust him. He bent down. She wrapped an arm around the back of his neck, as if she'd had a lot of practice. Roy hooked one arm under her back and the other behind her knees. He lifted, and began to walk with her through the trees.

He enjoyed carrying Joni this way. She was light enough so it caused little strain. Her arm reaching around his neck seemed almost friendly, though he knew she only did it for her own security. Her face was close to his. With a slight forward shift of his head, he could brush his cheek against the softness of her hair. The backs of her legs were bare against his right arm. As he walked, he caressed the velvety side of her thigh. Her free hand made no effort to stop him.

Soon a row of cabins came into view. They were painted like redwood, with slanted roofs. They had windows in back, but no doors.

Staying far away from the cabins, Roy worked his way past the end one. A break in the trees gave him a view of the parking area. It curved slightly southwards between the cabins. From its angle, he figured that the windows of the nearest cabin on the left should give him a view of all the other cabin fronts.

He made a wide sweep through the woods, and came up directly behind it. He grinned. The angle of the cabin's rear side shielded it from the other cabins. He set Joni on to her feet.

'What are you doing?' she whispered.

Whispered. He liked that.

'I'm getting us a place to stay.'

The window sill was level with Roy's head. The window was shut.

'I'm gonna lift you up,' he whispered. 'Tell me who's inside.' He put down his backpack and patted his shoulder.

Joni climbed on to his shoulders. She held the top of his head. Gripping her knees, Roy slowly stood until her eyes were level with the bottom of the window.

'Closer,' she said. She leaned forward, thighs pressing the sides of his head. Hands cupped to her eyes, she peered into the window screen. 'Higher,' she whispered.

He raised her. 'Who's there?'

'Nobody.'

'Are you sure?'

'Huh?'

'Is anyone there?'

'No.'

'You're sure?'

'Yes.'

He lowered her to the ground, and she climbed off. 'You're not lying, are you?'

'I don't tell lies,' she said solemnly.

'OK. You'd better not.'

'I'm hungry.'

'We'll eat when we get inside.'

'What?'

'I've got lots of stuff in the pack. But first we have to get in there.'

'How?'

He didn't answer. He led her to the right side of the cabin. There were two windows on the side, but they could be seen from the cabin across the parking area. He didn't want to chance being seen. They returned to the single rear window.

He could only get in by breaking it.

That would mean noise.

What were the alternatives? He could walk to the door of an occupied cabin, knock, and knife his way in. Someone might see him, though. And if he screwed it up there might be a scream. That'd be worse, by far, than a little breaking glass.

Maybe he should go under the cabin and watch for Donna from there. Kneeling, he looked into the crawl-space under the elevated floor. It was a couple of feet high. Plenty of room. He ought to have a good view from the front.

It would be filthy, though. All kinds of bugs and spiders. Slugs. Maybe even rats. No telling how long he would have to wait: maybe hours. And what would he do with Joni? The hell with that.

With his knife, he pried loose the two lower clamps of the window screen. He worked the screen loose and propped it against the wall.

Reaching into the pack, he took out his flashlight. 'OK,' he said, 'onto my shoulders.'

Joni climbed on.

Roy handed the flashlight to her. He straightened up. 'See up there? Where the window ends?'

'Here?' She pointed to the wood crossbeam at the bottom of the upper window.

'Right. Break the glass just above that, then you can undo the latch. Use the end of the flashlight. Hit it hard.'

'Here?'

'A little more to the left.'

'Here?'

'Yeah. Now hit it hard so it breaks the first time.'

Holding him across the forehead with one hand, she swung. Roy heard the loud slam of the flashlight striking glass. The glass didn't break. 'Hard!' he muttered. 'Hit it hard! Hard as you can.' He waited. 'Go ahead, damn it!'

The flashlight crashed down on his head. Again. Again. Pain streaked through his skull. He put a hand up. The flashlight struck his fingers.

Ducking, he rammed Joni into the wall. She cried out and dropped the flashlight. Roy reached up. He grabbed her blouse and tugged. The girl tumbled over his head. Her back slammed the ground.

'Hey!'

Roy looked towards the corner. A teenage girl stood there, holding towels in her arms.

'What the hell are you doing?' she demanded. She sounded more angry than afraid.

In an instant, Roy had his knife out. He pressed it to Joni's belly. 'I'm gonna kill this little girl if you don't come over here.'

'You wouldn't dare.'

'Run or yell, and I'll gut her like a catfish.'

The girl began to shake her head. 'You're sick,' she said.

'Come here.'

With short, hesitant steps, the girl began to approach

him. Her eyes watched him closely, as if trying to figure him out.

He watched how the late-afternoon breeze ruffled her hair. He watched how her small breasts jiggled seductively inside her white T-shirt. He watched her lean, tanned legs.

'What're you doing here?' he asked.

'I might ask you the same thing.'

'Just answer.'

'I own the place.'

'You?'

'My family.'

'Then you've got keys,' he said, and grinned.

# Chapter Eighteen

## 1.

Over the sound of the television, Donna heard a car drive up. Sandy looked at her, worried. Putting down the newspaper, Donna climbed off the bed and went to the window. A dark green Chrysler pulled to a stop just outside the door. 'It's Jud and Larry,' she said. She opened the door for them.

'Any sign of him?' Jud asked.

Donna shook her head. 'No. How'd you do?'

'Not too bad.'

'Not too bad, indeed!' said Larry. 'We got away scot-free, slick as thieves, and cast your eyes on *this*.' He waved a leather-bound book. '*This* is the diary of Lilly Thorn. Her own words. Good heavens, what a find!' He went to the edge of the bed and sat down beside Sandy. 'How was *your* afternoon, my little lady bug?'

Donna turned to Jud. 'Did you find the beast suit?'

'No.'

'What about Mary Ziegler's body?'

'Not that, either. There were a couple of places we couldn't search, though.'

'Did someone come back?'

'No. One of the rooms was already occupied, and we didn't check the cellar becuase there was a light down there.'

'Then somebody was home?'

'Several somebodies, by the looks of it.'

'There's only Maggie, Axel, and Wick,' she said.

'And two were over at Beast House running the tours.'

'So who was in the house?'

'Axel, I suppose. And at least two others.'

'But who?'

'I don't know.'

'That's a little spooky.'

'Yeah. I wasn't too happy about it, myself.'

They sat on the side of Jud's bed. 'What was the house like?' Donna asked.

She listened closely, intrigued by what he told her of the blue lights, the living room with no furniture except pillows, the bathtub with its strange handles. Most of all, she was fascinated by the bedroom.

'You wouldn't think Maggie Kutch was the type. And Hapson! That guy's an old weasel. It's hard to picture them making love at all, much less under mirrors. The bondage part I'll buy, though. The sadism. Did you see the look on his face when he went after Mary Ziegler with his belt?'

Jud nodded.

'I always thought they were a bunch of sickoes. I mean, you have to be, don't you, living on tours of a place like Beast House?'

# 2.

Except for a half-hour walk up a hill that overlooked the ocean, they spent the afternoon in Cabin 12. Larry read the diary in less than an hour, at times shaking his head in disbelief, and muttering. Sandy watched television. Donna sat next to the window with Jud.

At four-thirty, Donna mentioned that she'd like to find out about her car. The four of them walked to the Chevron station. As they approached it, she saw her blue Maverick along with three other cars parked beside the garage. 'I bet he hasn't touched it yet,' she said.

Jud walked with her to the office, where the bony mechanic was busy on the telephone. They waited outside until he was done.

'All set lady,' he announced, coming out.

'You mean it's ready?' Donna asked, unwilling to believe the surprising news.

'Sure is. Radiator came in around noon.' He walked ahead of them to the car and raised the hood. 'There she is. I test-drove her, and she runs sweet as a pie.'

They returned to the office. He showed her the bill, pointing out the cost of parts and labour. 'That be cash or charge?'

'Charge.' She searched her purse for the proper credit card.

'Where are you staying?' he asked.

'Over at the Welcome Inn.'

'That's what I figured. No place *else* to stay.' He took her credit card. 'That's what I told the fella looking for you.'

The words hit her hard. She stared at the man, stunned, until Jud's firm grip on her elbow brought her back. 'Who?' she asked.

'A fella come driving up in a '76 Rolls, says he knows your car. He find you?'

She shook her head.

'Do you always give out information about your customers?' Jud asked.

'Don't come up that often.' His eyes narrowed. 'You folks in some kind of trouble?'

'No,' Jud said, 'but you may be.'

The man handed the credit card back to Donna, then gave her the charge slips to sign. Slowly, he turned to Jud. 'Piss off, mister, before I kick your fucking ass from here to Fresno.'

'Shut up!' Donna shouted into his face. 'What right did you have to tell that man anything . . . *anything* . . . about me?'

'Hell, lady, I didn't tell him nothing. He had your name. He was gonna find you. Like I say, no place *to* stay but the Inn. He was gonna find you, anyway.' The mechanic flicked a hard glance at Jud, then looked back at Donna. 'Gonna step out on your husband, lady, you gotta be more careful.' He grinned and walked away.

'Let's go!' Donna called to her daughter and Larry. They were across the street looking in store windows. As they started back, Donna said, 'I don't want Sandy to know, OK?'

'She'll be more careful if she knows.'

'She's terrified of that man. And after what she's already been through, today . . .'

'We won't tell her. But we'll have to be damned careful from now on. Especially back at the Inn.'

Donna took his hand, and found confidence in his eyes. She met Sandy and Larry with a smile. 'Miracle of miracles,' she said. 'The car's fixed.'

3.

On the way back to the Welcome Inn, Donna wtched for a Rolls-Royce but didn't see one. There was no Rolls in the parking lot, either.

'Park in front of your cabin,' Jud said.

She did. Then Jud led them across the asphalt to his cabin. He entered first, and made a quick search before allowing them inside. 'I need to go to the office,' he said. 'I'll be back in a minute.'

He was back in less than five. With a slight shake of his head, he let her know that nobody had been asking about her at the office. 'Why don't we have supper now?' he suggested.

'I'm starving!' Sandy blurted.

'You're a bottomless pit,' Larry told the girl. 'An abyss.'

'*You're* the pit,' she said, laughing.

'Sandy,' Donna warned, 'don't use that kind of language.'

'*He* did.'

'That's different. He didn't mean 'pit' the way you did.'

'I most certainly did not.'

As they walked to the motel restaurant, Donna put her arm around Jud's back. Her hand touched a hard, jutting object just above his belt. She fingered the outline.

'So that's why your shirt tail's out.'

'Actually, it's out because I'm a slob.'

'A well-armed slob, at that.'

The dining room was nearly deserted. As the hostess led them among the tables, Donna checked every face. Roy wasn't there.

'We'd like a corner table, please,' Jud said.

'How's this?' asked the hostess.

'Just fine.'

Jud took a seat, Donna noticed, that would give him a wide view of the dining room.

A young, blond waitress came. 'Cocktails?'

Donna ordered a margarita.

Sandy asked for a Pepsi.

191

'I'd like a double martini,' Larry said. 'Very dry. Bone dry. In fact, dispense with the vermouth entirely.'

'So that's a double gin, straight up, with an olive.'

'Preicsely. You're a gem.'

'And you, sir?' she asked Jud.

'I'll have a beer.'

'Budweiser, Busch, or Michelob?'

'Make it Bud.'

'An incorrigible snob,' Larry muttered.

Donna laughed. She laughed very hard, harder than the remark deserved, but it seemed like a long time since anything had struck her as funny, and the laughter felt good. In a moment, a giggle escaped from Larry. That triggered Sandy. Soon the three of them were convulsed with mirth. Jud grinned at them, but his eyes kept sweeping the room.

During the whole dinner, Jud kept watch as if he weren't part of the group, but their guard. Then he insisted on paying the bill.

When they were leaving, Donna caught his arm and stopped him from following Sandy and Larry outside.

'What's . . .?'

'Thank you for dinner.' She hugged him tightly and kissed him. She could feel him begin to relax, to open, to let emotion into his kiss. Then he forced her away.

'We'd better stick close to Sandy,' he said, tearing down her good feeling so that she wanted to cry.

# Chapter Nineteen

From the window of the end cabin, Roy watched Donna, Sandy, and two men enter Cabin 12. Her car was parked in front of 9. He guessed that 9 was her place, and 12 the men's.

That simplified matters. Sometime during the night, Donna and Sandy would return to their cabin alone. Maybe in five minutes. Maybe not for hours. But sometime. Regardless, he would wait until after dark.

He looked around at the two beds, at the two girls tied to them and gagged. The older one, the owner's kid, was still sniffing. He figured she was sixteen, maybe seventeen. He didn't know her name. She'd been good, though. She'd been wet and slippery, and Roy suspected that she'd enjoyed herself. He'd spent nearly an hour with her after the four had walked off, probably for dinner. She hadn't started crying until afterwards. Guilt, more than likely.

He wondered why no one had come around looking for her. Maybe her folks were used to her disappearing.

Roy lifted an edge of the curtain, and looked again at Cabin 12. The door was still shut.

He looked around at the girls. Right now, he didn't want either of them. Still, they were nice to look at, lying there naked and powerless in the darkening room.

Later, maybe he could find time to take one of them.

Which?

Hell, he had lots of time to think about that. Lots of time.

He got up. The older girl's eyes watching him closely as he approached her. He bent over the bed. He traced a circle around her right nipple, watching the dark skin pucker and grow rigid. 'Like that?' he whispered, smiling down at her.

Then he jerked the pillow out from under her head, took it to the chair beside the window, and used it to cushion the straight wooden back. He sat down and leaned against the pillow. That felt much better.

He inched open the curtain and continued his watch.

# Chapter Twenty

## 1.

Leaving the others inside his cabin, Jud walked the perimeter of the Welcome Inn. He saw no Rolls-Royce nor any sign of a six-foot-two man who might be Donna's husband. He returned to his cabin. He motioned for Donna to come outside.

'Now,' he said, 'we'll go over to your place and wait for him.'

'What about Sandy?'

'Her, too.'

'Does she have to? I'd rather . . . I don't want her to see him, if it's possible.'

'Here's the problem. He doesn't seem to be around right now, but he might be. I could've missed him. If he's watching, he'll know we've left Sandy in 12. He might try for her.'

'Suppose she's with us,' Donna said, 'and Roy comes

and somehow he . . . gets by you. Then he's got Sandy. If we leave her with Larry and that happens, she'll still be all right.'

'Whichever way you want it.'

'Do you think he'll know, if we leave her in 12?'

'He might,' Jud admitted.

'But there's a good chance he won't.'

'I'd say so.'

'Okay. Let's leave her in 12 with Larry.'

'Fine.'

He instructed Larry to stay inside, to keep the door locked and the curtains pulled, and, at the first sign of trouble, to fire a signal shot and lock himself and Sandy in the bathroom. Low in the tub, they should be safe from bullets. Jud would come running. He'd be there five seconds after the first shot.

'Perhaps,' Larry said, 'I can pot the bugger with my signal shot.'

'If he gives you a clean shot, take it. But don't hang around waiting. You'll be fairly safe once you're in the tub with the bathroom door locked.'

Jud left him the rifle. He picked up Lilly Thorn's diary. Then he and Donna crossed the shadowy parking area to Cabin 9.

He went in first, and searched it. When Donna was in, he locked the door and made sure the window curtains were completely shut. He turned on the lamp on the nightstand between the two beds.

'Where do you want me?' Donna asked.

'I'll be on the floor here between the beds, so I'm out of sight. You might as well take one of the beds. Maybe this would be best,' he said, patting the one farthest from the door.

'Looks good to me. What'll we do while we wait?'

'You can watch TV, if you want. Doesn't matter I want to see what Lilly's got to say.'

'Can't I?'

'Sure.'

'Why don't I read it to you?'

'All right.' He smiled. He liked that idea. He liked it a lot.

Donna took off her sneakers. Her socks were white. Her feet looked very small to Jud. He watched her climb on to the bed and sit upright, bracing her back against the headboard.

He sat down on the floor between the beds. With a spare pillow, he padded the front of the nightstand, and leaned back. He placed his Colt .45 automatic on the floor beside him.

'All set?' Donna asked.

'All set.'

'"My Diary,"' she began to read. '"Being a True Account of My Life and Most Private Affairs."'

## 2.

'"January 1,"' she read. 'I guess this whole thing's 1903. "This being the first day of the new year, I devoted myself to solemn meditation. I gave proper thanks to the Lord for his bounty in providing me two fine boys, and the wherewithal to meet our needs. I asked Him to forgive my transgressions, but most of all to look kindly upon my dear Lyle, who had a fine noble heart and strayed from the path of righteousness only because he loved his family to a fault."'

'He was a bank robber,' Jud said

'But he had a noble heart.'

'Maybe you can skip some of this.'

'And get to the good part?' She slowly flipped the pages, scanning them. 'Oh, here's something. "February 12. I was sick at heart, today. The Lord continued to remind us that we are outcasts in this town. Several of the local youngsters attacked Earl and Sam as they were returning from school. The cowards wounded my boys with stones, then fell upon them, further bludgeoning them with fisticuffs and sticks. I know not the reason for their cruelty, only that its source lies in the reputation of the boys' father."'

Donna turned more pages. 'Looks like she went around town for a few days, telling the parents what their kids had done. They were polite to her, but cold. She no sooner got done making the rounds than her boys got beaten up again. One had a bad knock on the head, so she went to a Dr Ross. "Dr Ross is a kindly, cheerful man of forty-odd years. He appears to bear no grudge against myself or the children because of our kinship to Lyle. On the contrary, he looks upon us with the kindliest eyes I have seen in many months. He assured me that I need not fear for Earl's condition. I invited him to take tea, and we delighted in one another's company for the better part of an hour."'

Jud listened to the whisper of the turning pages.

'Looks like she's seeing Dr Ross almost every day. She's started calling him Glen. "April 14. Glen and I took a picnic basket to the hilltop behind the house. Much to my surprise and delight, he produced from his medicine case a bottle of the finest French Burgundy. We enjoyed ourselves marvellously, feasting upon chicken and wine, and upon each other's company. As the day progressed, our passion rose. I was hard put to restrain the man. Though he kissed me with an ardour that stole my breath away, I allowed him no further liberties."'

Donna stopped reading. She looked down at Jud, smiled, and sat down beside him on the floor. 'I'll allow you the liberty of a kiss,' she said.

He kissed her gently, and she pressed her mouth to his as if hungry for the taste of it. When he put a hand on her breast, she pushed it away.

'Back to Lilly,' she said.

Jud watched her skim the pages. She was sitting shoulder to shoulder with him, the book propped against her upraised knees. The soft downy hair on her cheek looked golden in the lamplight. The closeness and smell of her excited Jud so he stopped caring much about Lilly Thorn.

'She doesn't get very specific, but I think she's well beyond the kissing stage, at this point. She's hardly writing about anything, now, except Glen.'

'Mmmm.' Jud put a hand on Donna's leg, feeling the heat of her thigh through the corduroy.

'Ah-ha! "May 2. Last night, long after the children were abed, I stole outside at the appointed hour and met Glen in the gazebo. After many protestations of love, he asked for my hand in marriage. I accepted his offer without hesitation, and he joyously clutched me to his bosom. Through much of the night, we embraced and planned our future. At length, the chill became too great for us. We stole into the parlour. There, on the couch, we held one another tenderly, blessed by the fullness of the moment."'

Donna shut the diary, keeping place with her forefinger. 'You know,' she said, 'it makes me feel kind of . . . dirty, reading this. Like a peeping Tom, or something. It's so private.'

'It might tell us who killed her family.'

'It might. I'll go on with it. Only . . . I don't know.' She lowered her head and began turning the pages. 'They've set a date for the wedding. July 25.'

Jud put his arm across her shoulders.

'"May 8. We held another rendezvous in the gazebo, last night, meeting at the stroke of one. Glen had the presence of mind to bring a comforter. With the chill of night vanquished, our ardour burst upon us without restraint. We were caught as in a tide. Powerless to resist its pull, we allowed the tide to buoy us upon its bosom and sweep us into blissful delight such as I have never known." I guess,' Donna said, 'that means they screwed.'

'Christ, I thought their raft had capsized.'

Laughing, Donna pounded his leg. 'You're awful.'

She faced him, and he kissed her. 'Awful,' she said into his mouth.

He brushed his fingertips along the smooth skin of her cheek, traced the outline of her jaw and throat. She put the book down. Turning so a breast pushed against Jud's side, she plucked at his shirt, unbuttoning it. Then she slid her hand beneath it, stroking his belly and chest.

Jud pulled her down, away from the nightstand. Lying on his side, with the length of her pressed against him, he pulled her shirt tail free and slipped his hand down the back of her corduroys, feeling the cool smooth curves of her buttocks. He moved his hand up her back to unhook her bra.

'Wait,' she said.

'What's wrong?'

'The floor was last night,' she said, pushing away from him. She stood up.

With her eyes fixed steadily on Jud and a slightly apprehensive look on her face, she unbuttoned her blouse. She tossed it on to the bed near the door. She shrugged off her bra, and tossed it. Sitting on the side of the bed, she pulled off her socks. She stood, tugged open her belt, and unfastened her pants. They dropped to her ankles. She stepped out of them. Now she wore only brief panties. The dark of her pubic thatch was visible through sheer blue nylon. She slipped the panties off.

'Stand up,' she said. Jud noticed a tremor of fear or excitement in her voice.

He pulled off his shoes and socks. He set his Colt .45 beside the lamp. Then he stood, taking off his shirt. While he unbuttoned it, Donna unbelted his pants. She lowered them, kneeling. Then she slid the underpants down his legs. Her tongue licked and she took him in, sucking.

He moaned. As Donna stood, he brought her tightly against him. For a long time, he held her there between the beds, kissing her, exploring the slopes and crevices and orifices of her body, stroking and probing while she did the same with him.

Then they parted. Donna pulled back the covers, and they lay on the bed.

They didn't hurry.

Part of Jud's mind remained cautious, listening and alert like a guard standing watch. The rest of him joined Donna. He became part of her smoothness, her hair, the quiet sounds she made in her throat, her dry places and her slippery places, the many smells of her, the tastes. And finally the slick scabbard that took him, taunted him until he ached for release.

Arching his back, he thrust deeper, deeper than ever. Again. Crying out, Donna lurched up and grabbed him. He fell on her, ramming and ramming, and all the tight ache blasted out of him.

They lay together afterwards for a long time. They talked softly; they said nothing. Donna fell asleep holding his hand. Finally, Jud got up. He dressed, and resumed his position on the floor between the beds, the .45 automatic next to his leg.

## 3.

'Was I asleep long?' Donna asked.

'Half an hour, maybe.'

She pulled herself to the edge of the bed and kissed Jud. 'Want to get back to Lilly?' she asked.

'I've been waiting for you.'

'I really conked out.'

'Yeah.'

She smiled. 'All your fault.' She reached down a bare arm for the book.

'Maybe you'd better get dressed.'

'Mmmm.' She sounded as if she didn't care much for the idea.

'If we have a visitor . . .'

'God, did you have to remind me?'

He stroked the side of her face. 'You get dressed, and I'll look in on Sandy and Larry.'

'Okay.'

She covered herself with a sheet when Jud opened the door.

Sometime during their lovemaking, darkness had come. Light showed through the window of Cabin 12. Jud stood beside Donna's Maverick and searched the parking area. A woman with two children came out of Cabin 14. They got into a camper van. He waited for the van to leave, then he crossed to Cabin 12 and knocked lightly on the door. 'It's Jud,' he said.

'Just a sec.'

A moment later, Larry opened the door. Jud looked in. He saw Sandy sitting cross-legged in front of the television, looking over her shoulder at him.

'Everything okay?'

'Until you frightened the heebie-jeebies out of me a second ago, everything was marvellous.'

'Okay, I'll see you later.'

He went back to Donna's cabin. She was sitting on the floor between the beds, dressed in her cords and blouse, the diary resting against her upthrust knees. He sat down beside her, and put his .45 next to his right leg. 'They're fine,' he said.

'Okay. Back to Lilly. If you remember, her boat has just capsized.'

'Right. And she was drowned in waves of passion.'

'Which gave you the idea of making waves of your own.'

'Is that what happened?'

'I think so.'

Jud kissed her quickly, and she smiled.

'None of that,' she said. 'Back to Lilly.'

'Back to Lilly.'

'Okay, after she made it with Glen that first night, they "indulged their passion" on a regular basis. Almost every night, in fact. I don't suppose you want to hear about that.'

'In my present condition, not especially.'

'Okay, let's see what's next.' She turned several pages as she skimmed them. '"May 17. Today, I posted a letter to Ethel, requesting her attendance at the nuptials. I am hoping she will, at long last, journey down from Portland . . ."' Donna read the rest to herself and flipped the page. She remained silent. Looking up at her, Jud saw her eyes moving over the words. Her lips were pressed tightly together.

'What is it?' he asked.

Her eyes met Jud's. 'Something's happened,' she muttered.

'"May 18. A most disturbing sight greeted me, this morning, when I went down cellar to fetch a jar of apples from among those I'd put up last autumn. In the light of my gas lamp, I saw that two of my canning jars lay broken on the floor. Another was open as nice as can be, and empty. My first inclination, naturally, was to blame the boys. However, the label of the empty jar told me it had contained beets, a vegetable abhorred by both boys. That discovery chilled me to the heart, for I knew that a stranger had trespassed within my house and I knew not the nature of his intentions. Resisting my impulse to run upstairs and have done with it, I searched the confines of the cellar.

'"In a corner near the east wall, hidden from view behind half a dozen bushel baskets, I discovered a hole in the dirt floor – a hole large enough to permit the passage of a man or large animal. I quickly fetched my canned apples, and fled the cellar.

'"May 19. I gave much thought to informing Glen of the stranger's visit to my cellar. At length, I decided to leave him in ignorance, for I know that his protective instincts would call upon him to destroy the visitor, I could hardly abide such a stern measure. The visitor, after all, has thus far harmed no one.

'"I resolved to settle the matter myself, by covering the entrance hole. To accomplish this task, I fetched a spade from the tool shed. I went down to the cellar. Two more jars of preserves lay open and empty on the floor. This time, the visitor had indulged himself upon my peaches. Gazing down upon the empty jars, I felt a sudden warmth of compassion in my heart.

'"The visitor, I realized, meant me no harm. His only wish was to stave off the ravages of hunger. Perhaps he was an unfortunate lad, one of society's outcasts. I have known the pains of being an outcast. I have known the loneliness and the fear of it. My heart went out to the luckless, desperate soul who had dug into my cellar for a few mouthfuls of my preserves. I vowed to meet him, and help him if I can.

'"May 30." That's an eleven-day gap, Jud.'

'Yeah.'

'"May 30. I hesitate, I tremble, at the thought of committing my deeds to paper. To whom can I confide, however? Reverend Walters? He would only confirm that which I know already, that my deeds are foul in the eyes of God and I have condemned my soul to everlasting flames. I surely cannot tell Dr Ross. I know not what terrible vengeance he would certainly visit upon me and Xanadu.

'"On May 19, I resolved to meet and attempt to help the visitor to my cellar. Glen came by, after the children were abed. He used me after his usual fashion." What became of the surging tides?' Donna asked. She immediately continued reading. '"When he was done with me, we chatted idly for a time. At length he departed.

'"I went to the pantry, and silently opened the cellar door. There in the darkness, I waited, listening. Not a sound issued from the cellar. I descended the stairs, feeling my way cautiously, though I carried an unlighted lamp.

'"When I felt the dirt floor of the cellar under my bare

feet, I sat down upon the lowest step and continued my wait.

'"My patience, at length, was rewarded. A muffled sound of one breathing heavily with exertion rose from the vicinity of the hole. Soon came faint sounds such as a body might make dragging itself over hard earth. Then I saw a head appear above the bushel baskets.

'"The darkness concealed its features. I could only discern the head's pale shape. Even that was far from distinct. I judged it from the paleness to be the head of a man foreign to the blissful rays of the sun.

'"He rose to his full height, and I was filled with dread, for this was no man. Nor was he an ape.

'"As he drew near, I resolved to discover his identity more fully, even at hazard to my safety. To this purpose, I struck a match. It flared, giving me a momentary view of his hideous countenance before he cowered away, snarling.

'"While he was thus turned, I beheld his back and hindquarters. Whether he was one of God's exotic creatures, or an ill-made perversion vomited forth by the devil, I know not. His ghastly appearance and nudity shocked me. Yet I was drawn, by an irresistible force, to lay my hand upon his misshapen shoulder.

'"I allowed the match to die. In the darkness, totally without sight, I felt the creature turn. His warm breath on my face smelled of the earth and wild, uninhabited forests. He lay his hands upon my shoulders. Claws bit into me. I stood before the creature, helpless with fear and wonder, as he split the fabric of my nightgown.

'"When I was bare, he muzzled my body like a dog. He licked my breasts. He sniffed me, even my private areas, which he probed with his snout.

'"He moved behind me. His claws pierced my back, forcing me to my knees. I felt the slippery warmth of his flesh press down on me, and I knew with certainty what he was about. The thought of it appalled me to the heart, and yet I was somehow thrilled by the touch of him, and strangely eager.

'"He mounted me from behind, a manner as unusual for humans as it is customary among many lower animals. At the first touch of his organ, fear wrenched my vitals, not for the safety of my flesh but for my everlasting soul. And yet I allowed him to continue. I know, now, that no power of mine could have prevented him from having his will with me. I made no attempt to resist, however. On the contrary, I welcomed his entry. I hungered for it as if I somehow presaged its magnificence.

'"Oh Lord, how he plundered me! How his claws tore my flesh! How his teeth bore into me! How his prodigious organ battered my tender womb. How brutal he was in his savagery, how gentle in his heart.

'"I knew, as we lay spent on the earthen cellar floor, that no man – not even Glen – could ever stir my passion in such a way. I wept. The creature, disturbed by my outburst, slipped away into his hole and disappeared."'

### 4.

'"The following night, when I descended the cellar stairs, I found him waiting for me. I disrobed immediately to save my gown from the ravishment of his claws. I embraced him, savouring the slick heat of his skin. Then I went to my hands and knees, and he took me with no less fervour than on the previous night. When the delirium was past, we lay about until I recovered.

'"At length, I showed him my lamp. I indicated for him to turn around to protect his eyes. Then I lit the lamp, and covered it with an indigo hood I had devised during the day. The blue-shaded lamp was kind to his delicate eyes, while it provided sufficient light for my purpose.

'"I saw, as I studied him, that he was a curiously

shaped creature, indeed. Several of his odd features accounted, no doubt, for his magnificence as a lover. His lengthy, spearlike tongue was one of these. His sexual organ, without question, was the most singular and wondrous of his features, accounting as much for his ardour as for my own. Not only was it staggering in size and in its unusual contours and ridges, but also its orifice was unlike that of any creature known to me. The orifice, was hinged like a jaw, possessed a tongue like member with a two-inch extension."'

'Bullshit,' Jud said. 'What the hell is she trying to hand us?'

'A penis with a mouth?' Donna suggested.

'It's not such a bad idea?' Jud said, and laughed tersely.

'As long as it hasn't got teeth,' said Donna.

'Good Christ, how much of this is she making up?'

'What do you think?'

'I don't know. A lot of what she says – the claws and slippery skin, the reaction to light – they fit what I've seen.'

'What about the penis?'

'I didn't notice. Of course, the house was dark. I could hardly see anything.'

'I'll go on. "This orifice and tongue, I am certain, enabled him not only to titillate me in the extreme, but also heighten his ardour by the taste of my juices."'

'Good God!' Jud muttered, shaking his head.

'"After I satisfied my curiosity regarding his body, he explored me with much the same intensity. We then surrendered to a new tide of passion.

'"When we finished, I presented him with an assortment of food. He ate cheese with great delight. He nibbled the roll, and discarded it. He rejected the beef with barely a sniff. As I would later learn, only raw meat suited his palate, and this had been well cooked. He lapped water from a bowl, then sat down on his haunches, apparently satisfied.

' "Lying upon my back, I opened myself to him. He appeared confused, for he was accustomed to having his way in the manner of lower creatures. I urged him down upon me, however, so that I could look upon the strange beauty of his face and feel his slick flesh against my breasts as he ravished me.

' "When we were done, I watched him slide into the hole behind the bushel baskets. I crawled to the edge of the hole. I listened, hearing him deep inside. I called out quietly to him. I knew not what his name might be, so I called him Xanadu after the strange and exotic land described by Mr Coleridge in his unfinished masterpiece. He was gone, but I knew he would return the following night.

' "I have been with Xanadu every night, making my way very silently down cellar after the children are asleep. We indulge our passions with a frequency and intensity that knows no bounds. Each morning, before dawn, Xanadu returns to his hole. I know not why, nor where he goes. It is my belief that he is a creature of the night, who spends his days in sleep. I have become much that way myself.

' "Daylight finds me weary through every fibre. This has not gone unnoticed by Earl and Sam. I explain to them, with some truth, that I have found sleep difficult of late.

' "Glen Ross was my chief worry, in the beginning. He immediately expressed concern over my lassitude. He demanded to examine me for a physical ailment, but I resisted him to the point of rudeness. He surrendered his demand, and gave me sleeping powders.

' "His nightly demands for amorous attention aggravated and frightened me beyond telling. His embrace made me shudder. His kisses were repugnant to me. Yet I would have borne these tortures and allowed him liberties only to allay his suspicions had it not been for the visible evidence left on my body by Xanadu: the bruises, the scratches and cuts from his claws, the bite marks. Below my neck, hardly an inch of my body had not been wounded in the passion of our love. In the presence of my children and Dr Ross, I wore a high-necked blouse with long sleeves, and a full skirt. Even these were not sufficient covering. Upon one occasion, I attributed scratches on my hands and face to a tomcat flying into a rage when I picked it up.

'"Three nights ago, Dr Ross called on me and demanded to know the meaning of my icy rejections. Though I had long expected such an outburst, I was hard put to the answer in a manner that would bring no suspicion of the truth. At length, with a show of modesty and shame, I divulged that our sins of fornication placed our souls in jeopardy and I could no longer abide such evil. To my astonishment, he suggested that we marry at once. I said I could not live with a man who has brought such a fall upon me. With derisive laughter, he pointed out that I had been satisfied enough, living with a bandit and a murderer. I used this slur upon my deceased husband as a pretext to usher Dr Ross from the house. I do not think he will return.

'"Yesterday, I posted a letter to Ethel. I informed her that Dr Ross had taken back his marriage proposal, and that I was heartsick. I asked that she keep Sam and Earl for two weeks, so that I might make a restorative trip to San Francisco. I am now eagerly awaiting her reply. With the boys far off in Portland, I will be able to abandon my tiring pretences. Xanadu and I will have free reign of the house.

'"June 28,"' Donna read. 'That's what, almost a month after the last entry? "Tomorrow the children are due to return from Portland in the company of Ethel, who wishes to visit for an unspecified period. I have been looking forward with pain to their return.

'"For close on to three weeks, Xanadu and I have been alone in the house. With the arrival of others, he must return to the cellar. I know not whether my heart will bear such separation.

'"July 1. Last night while Ethel and the children slept, I visited the cellar. Instead of greeting me with an embrace, Xanadu glowered from the corner near his hole. He took the raw beef I offered him. Clamping it in his jaws, he crawled into the hole and disappeared. Though I waited until dawn, he did not return.

'"July 2. Xanadu has not returned.

'"July 3. Again tonight, he stayed away.

'"July 4. If he is trying to destroy me by his absence, he is succeeding. I know not what I will do if he does not return soon.

'"July 12. Ten nights have passed, and I fear he has no intention of returning. I know, now, that I was a fool to allow him up from the cellar. He grew accustomed to the comfort of the house, and my constant presence. How could he understand the necessity of his return to the cellar? How could he view it as anything other than rejection?

'"July 14. Last night, instead of keeping my vigil in the cellar, I wandered the wooded hills behind the house. Though I found no sign of Xanadu, I shall search again tonight.

'"July 31. My night time searches of the hillside have accomplished nothing. I am so weary. With the loss of Xanadu, all joy has passed from my life. Even in my children, I take no happiness. I resent them, with all my heart, for they were the instruments of my loss. I would certainly have torn them unborn from my womb, had I known the agony their presence would bring.

'"August 1. I spent last night in the cellar, hoping for Xanadu's return. I would have prayed, but I dared not insult the Lord in such a manner. I determined, at length, to end my life.

'"August 2. Last night, I waited until Ethel and the boys were asleep. Then I carried a length of rope down to the cellar. Lyle had often spoken to me of execution by hanging. It was a style of dying he dreaded until the day he was gunned down. I would have chosen a different way to end my life, but none seemed so sure as the hangman's noose.

'"I worked long on the rope, but was unable to devise a proper hanging knot. A simple loop, I decided, would make do. The pain of suffocation would be great, but only for a time.

'"I managed, after a great deal of trouble, to throw the loop over one of the cellar's support beams. I fixed the rope's loose end to the centre post. Then I climbed upon a chair that I had brought down cellar for that purpose. With the loop around my neck, I prepared myself for the end.

'"At length, I knew that I could not depart this life without making one final attempt to see my beloved Xanadu.

'"To this end, I stepped down from the chair and walked close to the mouth of his earthen hole. I knelt at its edge. I called out to him. Hearing no response after a wait of several minutes, I determined to seek him out. If I should perish in the attempt, so be it. Such an end would only save me from the pain of hanging.

'"Shedding my clothes, I climbed head-foremost into the hole, much as I had seen him do on so many occasions. The earth was cold and moist against my bare flesh. Its blackness was complete. The close confinement of the hole rendered crawling impossible, so I inched forward like a snake, flat on my belly. I know not how I struggled to writhe my way deeper. The walls of the tunnel seemed to tighten around me, bearing down as if to crush the breath from my lungs. Yet I forced myself onward.

'"When I could move no more, I cried out to Xanadu. I cried out in all the pain of my love and desperation. I cried out again and again, though every breath burned my lungs, for I loathed to die without bidding farewell to my lover.

'"At length, I heard the welcome sound of his slick flesh gliding through the clay. I heard the hiss of his breath. He pushed his snout against my face, moaning and licking.

'"Clenching my hair with his massive jaws, he propelled himself backward, dragging me. The pain of it was welcome to my dazed senses. When finally he released my hair, I found no more walls pressing in upon me. The air tasted fresh. I learned, later, that he had brought me to his underground dwelling, a hollowed-out space only large enough for him to stand upright and lie down, located just beyond the limit of my property and several feet beneath the earth's surface. The fresh air came from a concealed opening overhead, and other tunnels that led up the hillside. I learned all this in the morning, however. At the time Xanadu brought me to his dwelling, I was barley conscious, and trembling with chill. In my lover's embrace, the chill departed. I was wrapped in blissful sleep.

'"He woke me, sometime before dawn. I was much recovered. Xanadu entered my body, and loved me more gently than ever before, though not without an extreme of passion. When we were done, he led me to an opening. From the manner of our parting, I know that he will come to me tonight.

'"I made my way across the dewy grass, alone and naked in the early-morning grey.

'"I spent the morning in solitude, planning. Shortly before noon, my thoughts were interrupted by a young man named Gus, who wished to work for a meal. Firewood required splitting, so I gave him the job. For much of the afternoon, I heard the ring of his sledge. All the while, I planned.

'"It is evening, now. Gus took supper with us, and left. The children sleep. Ethel has not yet retired, but that is no matter. Xanadu waits. I shall allow him up from the cellar, and we will again have full reign of the house."

'That's it?' Jud asked.

Donna nodded.

# Chapter Twenty-one

Anytime, now.

In the dim light filtering through the curtain, Roy dressed. He got up and looked at the girls. Their skin seemed very dark against the white of the sheets.

He wanted to start a fire. It would take care of the girls, and whatever evidence he might be leaving behind. A fire would be perfect. But not without a delayed start.

He had no candles.

A cigarette or cigar might work as a delaying device, but he didn't have one.

Maybe the girl.

Crouching over her small pile of clothes, he lifted the T-shirt. It had no pockets. He picked up the cut-off jeans and searched their pockets. Nothing.

Shit!

He couldn't just set the room on fire and run: he had to give himself time. Time to get into Cabin 12, time to get into 9, time to get a good distance away in Donna's car.

Wait.

Shit, he'd have to burn 9 and 12, too.

Forget it.

Forget the whole thing.

He suddenly smiled. Without a delayed fire ready to set this place ablaze, he wouldn't have to rush. He could take his time, enjoy himself.

What he'd do, he'd wipe the place clean, make sure he left no prints.

He wandered the room with the girl's T-shirt, rubbing all the surfaces he remembered touching. Somehow, it seemed pointless. He wasn't sure why, but he felt a hollow ache in his stomach as if something had gone very wrong. Something he'd forgotten about.

He dumped the backpack on to the floor. Along with the ground cloth and sleeping bags, four cans of chilli and spaghetti rolled out.

He should've eaten. That's what made the ache.

He rubbed the cans with the T-shirt.

No, it wasn't just hunger. Something else was wrong.

He rubbed the aluminium tubing of the pack frame.

Shit!

Karen and Bob's place! He'd never found out, for certain, whether or not it had burned.

That morning, on the radio, they'd only mentioned the one fire. If Karen and Bob's place didn't go up, then the cops would have all the proof they'd need.

Okay, maybe it went up, and he just hadn't heard. He should still be careful with this place.

Not leave evidence.

Not leave witnesses.

He swept the room with his eyes, wondering if he'd missed anything. When he was satisfied the place was clean, he went into the bathroom and urinated. He came out. Bending down, he raised his cuff and slipped the knife from its sheath.

A single clean slash across the throats would do it. He'd stand back to stay out of the spray.

Knife in hand, he stood.

He took one step towards Joni's bed and realized she was gone.

Impossible!

Rushing to the bed, he slid his hands across its sheets to be certain his eyes and the darkness hadn't deceived him. No, the bed was empty. She'd somehow worked the rope loose.

He glanced down between the beds. No sign of her.

Under the bed?

The doorknob rattled. Roy looked, saw the small girl reaching, pulling. The door flew open for a moment, and shut.

'Oh fuck!' Roy muttered.

He ran to the door, swung it open, and stepped out. He shut it silently. Except for a few lighted cabin windows, the parking lot was dark. Roy looked to the left, thinking she would head for the office. No sign of her. He glanced to the right. Still nothing. Maybe she'd run around back.

'Okay,' he whispered. 'Okay.'

He would just finish off the other one, first.

He tried to twist the knob. It resisted, as if frozen.

Locked out. Keys inside.

Roy drew a deep, shaky breath. He wiped the sweat off his hands, then hurried around the corner of the cabin. Ahead was only darkness. Woods. The night sounds of crickets.

He wanted his flashlight.

He'd left it inside.

Walking quietly, he entered the darkness to find Joni.

The little bitch!

His hand ached, gripping the knife so hard.

He'd rip her! God, he would rip that little bitch! Up one side, down the other.

'Where are you?' he muttered. 'Think you can hide from me, little bitch? I know your smell. I'll sniff you down.

# Chapter Twenty-two

## 1.

'That's it,' Donna said. 'Lilly let the beast into the house, so it would kill the children and Ethel.'

'That's how it looks,' Jud agreed.

'It's not the way Maggie told it on the tour. Maggie had her barricaded in the bedroom, remember?'

'I think,' Jud said, 'that Maggie lies a lot.'

'Do you suppose she lied about Lilly going mad?'

'I doubt it. That's too easy to check on. We just need to see a local newspaper from the time to verify that. Lilly probably did flip out. If she was really behind the murder of her own children, that could send her over the edge. From the sound of it, she wouldn't have needed more than a nudge, at that point.'

'And watching Xanadu kill the children gave her the nudge.'

'Likely.'

'I wonder what Xanadu did after she was gone. Do you think he stayed in the house?'

'He might've. Or maybe he went off, and continued the way he'd lived before Lilly.'

'But he did come back,' Donna said, 'when Maggie and her family moved in. Maybe he was waiting, all that time, for Lilly to return. When he finally saw someone living there, he must've thought she'd come back.'

'I don't know,' Jud said. 'I really don't know what to think about any of this. The diary sure throws a monkey wrench into my theory about the beast. Assuming the diary is authentic. And I think we *have* to assume it's authentic, at least to the extent that Lilly Thorn wrote it. Nobody else had any reason to tell a story like that.'

'What about Maggie?'

'She kept it locked up. If she'd written it herself, faked it, she would've used it somehow: had it published, sold copies on the tour, something. I think she kept it for her own personal . . .'

A knock on the door silenced Jud. He picked up his automatic. 'Ask who it is,' he whispered.

'Who's there?'

'Mommy?' The girl's voice was choked with fear.

'Open it,' Jud said.

As Donna got to her feet, Jud lay down flat in the space between the beds.

He watched her unlock the door and pull it open. Sandy was standing in the darkness – standing on tiptoes to ease the pain of her pulled hair, tears shiny in her eyes, a six-inch blade pressed to her throat.

'Aren't you glad to see me?' a man asked, and laughed. He pushed Sandy ahead of him into the room, and kicked the door shut.

'Tell your friend to come out,' he said.

'There's no one.'

'Don't shit me. Tell him to come out, or I'll start cutting.'

'She's *your daughter*, Roy!'

'She's just another cunt. Tell him.'

'Jud!'

He pushed his pistol under the bed, and slowly stood, hands out to show they were empty.

'Where's your piece?' the man asked.

'Piece?'

'Everybody's playing dumb. Cut the fuckin' dumb show, and tell me where's your gun.'

'I don't have a gun.'

'No? Your buddy did.'

'Who?'

'Shit.'

'Who're you?' Jud asked.

'Okay, knock it off. Both of you, get your hands on top of your head and interlace your fingers.'

'Donna, who is this guy?'

'My husband,' said Donna, looking confused.

'Jesus, why didn't you tell me? Look, fella, I didn't even know she was married. I'm sorry. I'm really sorry. You think *you're* mad, my wife's gonna kill me. You aren't gonna tell her, are you? Why don't you put down that blade, man? The kid didn't do nothing. She didn't know from Adam. We just stuck her on this guy, gave him a couple of bucks to babysit while we . . . you know, had a good time.'

'Get over against the wall, both of you.'

'What're you gonna do? You're not gonna . . . hey, we didn't even *do* nothing! I didn't even touch her. Did I touch you, Donna?'

Donna shook her head.

'See?'

'Face the wall.'

'Oh Jesus!'

'That's good. Now both of you brace yourselves against it. That's right. Lean. So your weight's on your hands.'

'Oh sweet Jesus!' Jud muttered. 'He's gonna kill us. He's gonna kill us!'

'Shut up!' Roy snapped. He made Sandy lie face down on the floor. 'Now don't move, kid, or I'll gut your mom.'

'Oh sweet Jesus!' Jud cried.

'You shut up.'

'I didn't touch her. Just ask her. Donna, did I touch you?'

'Shut up,' Donna said.

'Jesus, everybody's turning on me!'

'He's already killed at least two people,' Donna said, 'and we're gonna be next if you don't shut up.'

'He *killed* somebody?' Jud looked over his shoulder at the man stepping towards him with a knife. 'You really killed somebody?'

'Face front.'

'He killed my sister and her husband.'

'You did?' Jud asked, looking again.

The man's grin told how much he had enjoyed it.

Jud began to turn, asking, 'Why'd you . . .?'

'Face front!' Roy reached forward to shove Jud into position. As his hand thrust Jud's shoulder, Jud reached back with his right hand, pressed Roy's hand flat against his shoulder, and spun out. Roy yelped as his wrist snapped. Jud, still pivoting, smashed a forearm into the back of Roy's head, slamming him against the wall. In the same swift motion, he hammered his knee into Roy's spine. The knife dropped to the floor. Roy fell backward, groaning, panic in his eyes.

'Take Sandy over to 12,' Jud said. 'See what happened to Larry.'

## 2.

Outside, Donna crouched and hugged her crying daughter. 'Did he hurt you, honey?'

She nodded.

'Where did he hurt you?'

'He pinched me here.' She pointed to her left breast, a barely noticeable rise through her blouse. 'And he put his finger down here.'

'Indeed?'

She nodded and sniffed.

'He didn't rape you, though?'

'He said later. And he used the bad word.'

'What did he say?'

'The bad word.'

'You can tell me.'

'He said later. He said later he'd F me till I can't walk straight. And then he was gonna F you. And then he was gonna gut us like catfish.'

'Bastard,' Donna muttered. 'The stinking bastard.' She held Sandy gently, stroking the girl's head. 'Well, I guess he won't get a chance to do any of that, will he?'

'Is he dead?'

'I don't know. But he can't hurt us now. Jud took care of that.' She stood. 'Okay, let's see about Larry.'

'Larry's okay. I tied him real good.'

'*You* tied him?'

'I had to. Daddy was gonna kill him.'

They started walking across the parking area.

'I told Daddy, if he killed Larry, I'd scream. He said he'd kill me if I did, and I said I didn't care. I said, if he didn't kill Larry, I'd do anything he wanted. He wanted me to pretend so he could make you open the door.'

'How did he get *Larry* to open the door?'

'He pretended to be a policeman.'

'Great,' Donna muttered, wondering how Larry could be that stupid. She tried the door of Cabin 12. It wasn't locked. She pushed it open.

'Where is he?'

'In the bathtub. It was Daddy's idea.'

She found Larry facedown in the empty tub, a shirt tied around his mouth for a gag. His hands were bound together behind his back, and knotted to the ankles of his upraised feet.

'We got him!' Sandy announced.

Larry answered with a grunt.

Sitting on the edge of the tub, the girl leaned forward and picked at the knots. In a few moments, she had them loose. Larry pushed himself to his knees. He tugged the knotted shirt down from his face, and plucked a black sock out of his mouth. 'Dreadful man,' Larry muttered. 'A total barbarian. Are both of you all right? Where's Judgement? What happened?'

Donna explained what Jud had done, and that she didn't know how badly he'd injured Roy.

'Perhaps we should find out.'

They crossed through the darkness to Cabin 9 and found Jud sitting on the bed. On the floor between the beds, Roy lay face down. His hands were tied behind his back. A pillowcase covered his head, strapped tightly around his neck with a leather belt. Except for his breathing, he was motionless.

'I see you have matters well in hand,' Larry said.

Sandy, looking down at her father, squeezed Donna's hand tightly. Donna sat down beside Jud. They moved sideways to make room for the girl.

'What shall we do with the cad?' Larry asked, lowering himself daintily on to the empty bed.

'He's not a cad,' said Jud. 'He murdered Donna's sister. He murdered her brother-in-law. He sexually abused Sandy. God knows what else he's inflicted on Donna and Sandy. But we all know what he intended to do. That's not a cad, in my book. In my book, that's a beast.'

'What do you propose we do with him?' Larry asked.

'Put him where he belongs.'

'In jail?' Sandy asked.

Donna, feeling a chill scurry up her back, said, 'No, honey. I don't think that's what Jud has in mind.'

Larry suddenly understood. Shaking his head, he muttered, 'Oh dear God.'

# Chapter Twenty-three

Donna started the engine of the Chrysler. Beside her sat Sandy. Roy, his head still hooded by the pillowcase and his hands still bound, sat in the back between Jud and Larry. Jud held a .45 against Roy's chest. Larry held a machete across his lap, its curved head pressing Roy's side.

'Once you let us off,' Jud said, 'I want you to drive back to the motel. Give us half an hour, then come back for the pick-up. If we're not waiting, don't stick around. Take off, and come back every fifteen minutes until we show. Any questions?'

'Can't I just park somewhere close, and wait? Then I can signal if someone comes.'

'The car might attract notice.'

'Are they really going in Beast House?' Sandy asked, as if it were a joke everyone was in on except her.

'I guess so,' Donna answered.

'That's crazy.'

'It certainly is,' Larry agreed. 'I concur 100 per cent.'

'You don't have to come,' Jud said.

'Oh, but I do. You are planning to rid the world of Lilly's beast, I take it?'

'I'm planning to.'

'Well, if I'm to bear the expense of the operation, I certainly want to see it carried out. Besides, you may need a hand with our friend here.'

'Are you taking Daddy in there, too?'

'Yes,' Jud said, and didn't explain.

'What for?'

'Punishment.'

'Oh. You're gonna give him to the beast?'

'That's right.'

'Wow! Can we go in too?' she asked Donna. 'I want to see.'

'No, we can't.'

'Why not?'

'It's dangerous.'

'But Jud and Larry are going in.'

'That's different.'

'I want to. I want to see the beast get Daddy in its claws and rip him up.'

'Sandy!'

'I want to see it!'

'Take my word for it,' Larry said. 'You don't want to see the beast do that to a man. I know.'

'We're almost there,' Donna said.

'Okay. Drive on past it, then hang a U.'

'Here?'

'Go a bit farther, so we're past the bend.'

Donna slowed.

'This'll be fine.'

She tried to swing the big car into a U-turn, saw that she couldn't make it, and had to back up before finishing the turn.

'Okay,' Jud said. 'Now kill the lights.'

She pushed the headlight knob, and the road ahead

went dark except for patches of moonlight. The road was less dark than the woods on either side, so she had little trouble staying on it. Around the curve, the woods ended. The moon spread pale, creamy light over the road.

'Pull up in front of the ticket booth,' Jud said, his voice a tense whisper.

Donna stopped.

'I'll need the keys for a second.'

She switched off the ignition. Turning in her seat, she handed the key case to him. 'Jud?' she said.

His features were barely visible.

'Shouldn't we just take him to the police?'

'No.'

'It's not that I . . . Can't we shoot him, or something?'

'That'd be murder.'

'It'll be murder giving him to the beast.'

'Then the beast is the perpetrator, not us.'

'I don't want you going in that house again. Not at night. Christ, Jud!'

'It's all right,' Jud said quietly.

'It's *not* all right. You could get killed. It's not fair. We've only had two days.'

'We'll have plenty more,' he said, and climbed from the car. He dragged out Roy, who stumbled and dropped to his knees. 'Keep him here,' Jud told Larry.

Donna followed Jud to the trunk.

'Please,' he said, 'get in the car.'

'One kiss.'

'All right.'

She pressed herself tightly against him, squeezing him hard, hoping that somehow their bodies might fuse and she could stop him from leaving. But after a moment, he forced her gently away.

She watched him take his torn parka from the trunk and put it on. He picked up two flashlights and a road flare. Then he quietly shut the trunk and handed the keys to her.

225

'What time does your watch say?' he asked.

'Ten forty-three.'

He set his. 'Okay. Meet us here at eleven-fifteen.'

'Jud?'

'Go. Please. I want to get this done.'

She went back to the car, started it, and drove away without looking back at the three men she'd left along the roadside.

# Chapter Twenty-four

## 1.

'It's a turnstile,' Jud said. 'Climb over it.'

Roy shook his head.

Jud prodded him with the knife, and Roy swung a leg up. Larry, on the other side, helped him over by pulling one of his tied arms. Jud heard an approaching car. He vaulted the turnstile, grabbed Roy, and pulled the big man to the ground. The three of them lay close to the ticket-booth wall.

Jud heard the car slow. Its tyres crunched gravel. Crawling forward, he peered around the corner of the ticket booth.

A police car.

It was stopped across the road, but Jud could hear the quiet idle of its engine. A few moments passed. Then it made a U-turn, drove slowly by the ticket booth, and headed off.

They dragged Roy to his feet and led him up the lawn. They hurried alongside the house to the back. There, they climbed the porch stairs.

The broken glass in the back door had neither been replaced nor boarded over. Sliding the knife into his pocket, Jud reached through the opening. He lowered his fingers down the door crack until he found a bolt. He tried to draw it back. It was stuck. He jerked. It snapped back with a clatter that filled the silence.

'That probably woke it up,' Larry whispered.

Jud pushed open the door. He stepped inside, pulling the hooded man. Larry, following, shut the door without a sound.

'Where to?' he whispered.

'Let's take this off, first.' Jud removed the belt from Roy's neck, then pulled off the pillowcase. The man's head jerked as he looked quickly around.

'This is Beast House,' Jud told him.

He made noises through his nose.

'I'll take off the gag. You'll live a bit longer, though, if you stay quiet.'

Roy nodded.

Jud tore the adhesive tape off Roy's mouth, and pocketed it. He strapped the spare belt around his waist, and tucked in the pillowcase so it hung at his side like a white sash. He planned to leave nothing behind.

Nothing but Roy.

'Let's go upstairs,' he whispered.

'That's where the *monster* lives?' Roy asked, and laughed.

'That's where it usually attacks,' Jud said.

'Yeah? You believe that shit?'

'Shhhh.'

Jud stepped out of the kitchen. He flicked on his flashlight. Ahead was the entrance hall, its stuffed-monkey umbrella holder guarding the front door like a grotesque sentry. He put his light away. With his left hand, he reached under the back of his shirt and pulled the Colt automatic from his belt.

'What're you guys, trying to scare me?'

'Shhh,' Larry repeated.

'Shit.'

At the foot of the stairs, Roy said, 'I smell gas.'

'That's from last night,' Jud whispered.

'Yeah?'

'A woman was killed,' Larry said.

'No shit? You guys do this all the time?'

'Shut up,' said Jud.

'I was only making conversation.'

They started up the stairs, and last night's horrors filled Jud's mind: Mary Ziegler, dead, diving down at him; the liquid sounds she made rolling across his back; the awful stench of the beast. He looked towards the top of the stairs, half afraid he would see her there again.

'Anybody got a smoke?' Roy asked.

'Shut up.'

They reached the top of the stairs.

'Okay,' Jud said, 'lie down.'

'What?'

'Lie face down on the floor.'

'Fuck you.'

With a sudden kick, Jud knocked the left leg out from under Roy. The man sat down hard.

'Fuckin' bastard.'

'Face down.'

Roy obeyed.

'You just wait, motherfucker. I'll gut you like a catfish. I'll cut off your cock and jam it down . . .'

'In there,' Jud whispered to Larry, pointing to the door several feet from Roy.

'Alone?'

'Just a second.' Jud knelt. 'Okay, Roy. You just lie here quietly. I tell you what: if you make it to dawn alive, I'll turn you over to the cops.'

'Fuck you.'

'But the only way you've got a chance is to stay real still, and real quiet. Maybe you'll be lucky, and the beast won't notice you.'

'Fuck you.'

'We'll be right over there, where we can keep an eye on you. If you try to sneak off, I'll have to dump you. Any questions?'

'Yeah. What's your name? I like to know a guy's name before I gut him.'

'My name is Judgement Rucker.'

'Shit.'

Jud went to the door where Larry waited. Jud opened it. He flashed his light up its narrow stairway, to the door high overhead. 'This'll be good,' he whispered. 'We can sit on the stairs.'

They stepped inside. Jud put his flashlight away. He pulled the door towards him until only a crack remained. Eye close to the crack, he could see the shape of Roy lying on the dark corridor floor.

Jud switched the automatic to his right hand. With his left, he removed Roy's knife from the pocket of his parka. He patted the parka, feeling the good weight of his spare ammo clips.

'Judge?' Larry whispered. 'Will we actually let the beast have him?'

'Shhh.'

2.

Donna wanted to turn around, wanted to go back to Beast House and wait there for the men to finish. As she was about to make the turn, however, car headlights flashed on her rear-view mirror. The car drew quickly closer. Donna thought she could see a light rack on its roof. She checked her speedometer. No, she wasn't speeding.

Sandy looked back. 'Uh-oh,' she said.

'Yeah.'

'Are you gonna pull over?'

'Not unless he wants me to.'

'Why's he so close?'

'He hasn't got manners.'

The police car stayed on their tail all the way to the Welcome Inn. It followed them through the entrance, then angled left and parked beside the restaurant.

Sandy made an exaggerated, 'Whew!'

'I guess he was just hungry,' Donna said. She pulled into the parking space of Cabin 12. 'Let's give him a minute to get inside.'

'Then what?'

'We'll go back for Jud and Larry.'

'Jud said half an hour.'

'We'll be a little early.'

She backed up and headed out of the parking lot. With a glance at the police car, she saw it was empty. The policeman was nowhere in sight. She turned left.

'If we're early,' Sandy said, 'can we go in?'

'Are you out of your tree?'

'Maybe we can help Larry and Jud.'

'They'll be fine without our help.'

'I'm not scared of the beast.'

'Well, you *should* be.'

'We can take Jud's rifle in with us.'

'Bullets can't hurt it. Weren't you listening on the tour?'

'Sure.'

'Maggie said her husband shot it.'

'Hunh-uh. She only said she heard shots. He probably just missed.'

'Well regardless, we're not going anywhere near that house.'

The town seemed empty as Donna drove through it. A few cars sat in front of closed stores, as if deserted by drivers seeking shelter from the darkness. Street lights cast their glow on barren corners. The traffic light blinked a steady yellow caution.

Donna swung left across the road and pulled into a parking space in front of Arty's Hardware. The headlights glared off the display window. She shut them off. 'Can you see the house?' she asked.

Sandy peered out of the side window. 'Just the front yard.'

Donna, looking out the far side of the car, could see little except the front of the fence and the ticket booth. 'I guess I'll get out,' she said.

'Me too.'

'Okay.'

They shut the doors silently and met in front of the car. Their tennis shoes were quiet on the sidewalk. At the corner of the hardware store, they came to the wrought-iron fence.

Between the wall and the fence, a narrow walkway ran to the rear of the hardware store. A low picket gate blocked entry. Donna opened it, and they stepped into the gap. Close to the store wall, she felt well hidden from the street.

Sandy took hold of her hand.

Across the lawn, Beast House stood silent. Its board siding, washed by moonlight, looked as pale and dead as driftwood. Where overhangs and balconies dropped shadows, the black made caverns deep into the house.

Donna looked at the dark bay windows. She lifted her eyes to Lilly Thorn's bedroom windows, then along the bone-grey wall to Maggie's window, the one Larry had used for his escape so many years ago. In her mind, she could see the wax figure just inside, struggling to raise the window.

'What time is it?' Sandy whispered.

Donna tipped the face of her wristwatch to catch the moonlight. 'Eleven-twenty.'

'They're late.'

232

'That's all right.'
'What if they don't come out?'

### 3.

'Fuckin' shit!' Jud heard panic in Roy's voice. 'Holy fuckin' shit, there's someone coming! Guys? Damn it, you guys!'

Jud knelt, leaving space above him for Larry to see through the crack. Shifting the pistol to his left hand, he wiped his sweaty palm on a leg of his jeans. Then he pulled out his flashlight.

'Guys!' As if giving up on them, he muttered in a low voice, 'Oh Jesus.'

Jud heard a stair creak.

'Hey, who are you.? Huh? Can you help me? There's these two guys, they tied me up. I mean, I'm not trespassing. I been kidnapped. Can you give me a . . . oh shit. *Oh shit!* GUYS!'

Jud heard soft, brittle laughter.

'Oh God.' Roy was starting to cry. 'Oh God, sweet Jesus!' He sobbed. 'Oh Jesus, get it away! Get it away!'

Behind Jud, Larry moaned in horror.

Roy shrieked as the beast sprang. Its pounce seemed to knock out his wind, cutting his outcry short.

Jud shoved the door open. He aimed his flashlight. Flicked it on. The white, snarling thing on Roy's back snapped its head around to look. Bleeding flesh hung from its teeth.

Behind him, Larry screamed.

Before he could raise his automatic, Larry shoved him. He tumbled into the corridor. Larry, still screaming, leapt over him. Jud raised his flashlight. He shined it into the slitted eyes of the beast as Larry rushed it. He saw Larry swing. Saw the machete flash. Heard the thud of it and saw the white, hairless head tumble into the darkness. Blood spouted from the neck stump. The torso flopped on to Roy's back. Jud heard the muffled thumps of the head dropping from one stair to the next.

'I killed it,' Larry whispered.

Jud got to his knees.

'I killed it. Dead!' Larry swung the machete down like an axe, chopping into the dead creature's back. 'Dead!' He hacked it again. 'Dead dead dead!' After each word, he struck.

'Larry,' Jud said softly, standing up.

'I killed it!'

'Larry, we're done in here. Let's get out . . .' Behind him, Jud heard a savage snarl. He whirled. His flashlight reached up the attic staircase. The door at the top stood open. He dropped his beam to the massive, white back of a creature plunging down the stairs.

He snapped the trigger. His Colt roared, flashing as it bucked. A howl tore his ears. The beast took him backward, slamming him to the hallway floor. He jammed the gun muzzle against its side and shot. Another screaming howl. Then the weight was off him. He rolled to his stomach. The flashlight was still in his left hand. He found the white thing lunging at Larry, though two holes in its back poured blood. Larry raised the machete high. A sweeping arm caught the side of his face and raked the skin off. The machete fell.

Dropping the flashlight, Jud pulled the knife he'd taken from Roy. He scurried forward. In the dark, he saw the dim figure of the beast swing around, clutching Larry. Jud sidestepped. As his foot passed through space, he knew that he'd overstepped the top of the stairway. He dropped his knife and tumbled into the darkness.

# 4.

Donna listened, aghast, to the muffled outcries and gunshots coming from the house. She glanced down at Sandy. The girl stood transfixed, mouth gaping. At the crash of glass, she swung her eyes to the house in time to see a window of Maggie's bedroom explode as a body burst through it, head first.

No, not a body. The wax figure of Larry Maywood.

*But it's screaming!*

Moonlight glowed on the white hair of the plunging man. Another figure tumbled through the window. She watched it spin, its arms and legs frozen, and knew this one was only wax. Larry's scream stopped with the first thud of impact.

Without a word, Donna shoved open the low wooden gate and pulled Sandy behind her to the car. 'Inside. Get inside.'

'But Mom!'

'Do it!'

As Sandy got into the car, Donna hurried to the rear. She opened the trunk. Leaning in, she pulled a road flare out of its wrapper. She stuffed it into her rear pocket. Then she unzipped a leather case and slipped out Jud's rifle. She slammed the trunk lid. Pushing the rifle bolt forward, she watched a long, pointed cartridge slide into the chamber. She forced the bolt down and rushed to Sandy's window.

'Keep the doors locked and windows up till I get back.'

The girl gazed as if her mind were far away, but she locked the door and began rolling up her window.

Donna ran for the ticket booth.

# 5.

Halfway down the stairs, where Jud lay clutching a baluster, he heard the smash of glass and Larry's scream. Jud started climbing. The white creature appeared above him. It leapt. He fired one, point blank, before the claws hit his hand and tore the gun away. With an anguished screech, the creature shoved past Jud. It staggered down the stairs. Leaning over the bannister, Jud saw its pale shape moving towards the kitchen.

He hurried to the top of the stairs. Patting the floor near the bodies of Roy and the first beast, he found his flashlight. He turned it on. By its light, he found Larry's machete. He ran up the corridor to Maggie's bedroom. His light showed a broken window beyond the toppled, papier-mâché screen. Then it picked up a headless torso. He was crouching over the body when he realized it was only the wax figure of Tom Bagley, Larry's boyhood friend.

Jud ran to the window and looked down. Two sprawled bodies on the ground. A woman kneeling by one.

Donna.

'Is he alive?'

Donna's face tilted up. 'Jud are you okay?'

'Fine,' he lied. 'Is Larry alive?'

'I don't know.'

'For God's sake, get help. Get him a doctor. An ambulance.'

'Are you coming down?'

'I'm going after the beast.'

'No!'

'Get Larry help.' He pushed himself away from the window and crossed the room to the dresser. Shoving the machete under his belt, he tugged the top drawer open. The dead husband's Colt .45 automatic was just where Maggie had left it. Depressing a button, he dropped its empty clip. He took the oversized, twenty-shot clip from his pocket and rammed it up the handle. It locked into place. Priming a cartridge into the chamber, he ran from the room.

In the corridor, he stepped over the bodies and rushed downstairs. He ran into the kitchen. His flashlight picked up blood on the floor. He followed its trail to the pantry, through an open door, and down a flight of steep wooden stairs to the cellar.

The moist cellar air was chilly and smelled of earth. Sweeping the area with light, he saw stacks of bushel baskets, shelves laden with dusty canning jars. Out of curiosity, he abandoned the trail of blood and stepped closer to the baskets. Behind them, just as described in Lilly Thorn's diary, he found a hole in the dirt floor.

He returned to the dark blood spots on the dirt and followed them to the right where they stopped in front of an upright steamer trunk set flush against the wall. He saw quickly that the trunk was latched shut. The beast couldn't have hidden itself inside.

Two gunshots came, faint with distance. For a moment, he worried. Then he realized that Donna must've fired the rifle to draw attention, to draw the police and help for Larry.

Setting his flashlight on the dirt floor to the right of the trunk, he tucked the Colt into a pocket of his parka. He slipped his fingers between the trunk and the wall, and pulled. With a gritty scraping sound, the trunk came away from the wall. A rope handle dangled from the back of the trunk. The rope was dark with wet blood.

Where the wall should have been, Jud found a tunnel. Picking up the flashlight, he entered it.

# 6.

Realizing that Larry was dead, Donna ran to the front door of the house. She used two shots to blast apart the lock of the door. Even then, she had to throw her shoulder against the solid wood several times to smash it open. She stepped into the entry hall. 'Jud?' she called.

She heard no answer. She heard no sound at all. She called him again, louder this time. Still, no answer came.

Slinging the rifle over her shoulder, she slid the road flare out of her rear pocket. She twisted off its cap. Reversing the cap, she rubbed its striking surface against the end of the flare. At first, there was only a spark. On the second stroke, the flare sputtered to life, its brilliant blue-white tongue casting a glow that lit the entry hall and much of the stairway. Slowly, she climbed the stairs. She continued climbing, even when the light of her flare illuminated the bodies at the top: Roy face down, the nape of his neck mauled to red pulp; a strange white creature on Roy's back. When she saw the stump of its neck, she gagged. Turning away, she threw up.

Then she resumed climbing. She reached the top of the stairs and stepped over the bodies. She walked down the corridor to Maggie's bedroom, took one step inside, and called out, 'Jud!' She crossed the hall to Lilly's room, and again she called to him. Again, she got no answer.

She returned to the head of the stairs. Even with the beast lying dead at her feet, she felt an icy reluctance to venture down the corridor to the other rooms. 'Jud!' she yelled. 'Where are you?'

When no answer came, she walked quickly down the narrow hall. She shoved aside two of the Brentwood chairs marking the future Ziegler exhibit. At the far end, she stepped into the room to her left. The flare cast fluttering light on the walls, the rocking horse, the twin beds, and the wax figures of Lilly Thorn's slaughtered children. 'Jud?' she asked quietly. Nothing in the room stirred.

Crossing the hall, she twisted the knob of the nursery door. When it didn't give, she remembered Maggie saying it was always kept locked. She kicked it twice. 'Jud?' Then she muttered, 'Damn it.' She looked for a safe place to put the flare. Crouching, she propped it against the wall. The wallpaper began to blacken and curl. Standing, she unslung the rifle and shot through the crack where the lock tongue entered the jamb. She recocked it. Then she nudged the door with her shoulder. Feeling it give, she picked up the flare. She slung the rifle over her shoulder and shoved open the nursery door.

'Jud?' she called. She stepped into the room. Her flare lit an empty cradle, a playpen, a doll house nearly as high as her waist. It also lit buckets, a mop, three brooms, a carpet sweeper, and a table littered with sponges, rags, furniture wax, cleaning fluid, and window polish. Apparently, the nursery had been taken over by Axel for storage.

Donna backed out. She hurried through the corridor, past the Brentwood chairs, and stopped near the bodies.

She gazed at the door to the attic. It stood wide. 'Jud?' she called up the stairs.

She began climbing the stairs. They were very steep. The walls seemed close, as if they were pressing in on her. She hurried. Above her, the door stood open. She climbed to it, and hesitated before stepping inside. 'Jud, are you in here? Jud?'

She ducked through the low doorway. In the circle of light cast by her flare, she saw a rocking chair, a pedestal table, several lamps, and a sofa. She stepped away from the door. Moving sideways, she squeezed between the table and sofa. Ahead stood a weaver's loom. She skirted to the left of it, swung a leg over the high roll of a rug, and stumbled to keep from stepping on a hand. Catching herself against a chair she whirled around, saw wild hair, wide-open eyes, torn shoulder and breasts.

Not Jud, thank God.

Mary Ziegler.

From ankle to hip, little except bones remained of Mary's right leg. Donna turned away, doubled over, and vomited. Her stomach, already empty, kept convulsing, wracking her with pain. Finally, it stopped. She wiped the tears from her eyes and started back towards the door.

She stepped over the rolled rug. She pressed sideways between the table and the sofa. Then, just ahead of her, the door slammed shut.

# Chapter Twenty-five

## 1.

Jud made his way farther into the tunnel, crouching beneath its low ceiling, trying to fight off the sense of suffocation caused by its narrow walls. In places, the earth was shored up with boards. The work of humans.

Wick Hapson, maybe. Or Axel Kutch.

Jud knew, even before stepping into the tunnel, where it would lead him. But he hadn't realized it would be this far. For some reason, the tunnel was not straight. It meandered like an old river, with twists and loops, and hairpin turns. At one point, it split into a Y. Jud went left. The tunnel curved, rejoined the other branch, and continued towarf the west.

At every turn, his finger tensed on the pistol trigger ready for an abrupt assault by the wounded beast. But rounding each, he saw only more tunnel and another bend.

Soon he began to wonder if he had somehow passed the opening he'd expected to find. He remembered the Y. Perhaps the right-hand branch led past the house entrance before curving back to join the one he'd taken.

That seemed unlikely. Still . . .

He stepped around a bend, and the tunnel opened. With a sweep of his flashlight, he found himself in a cellar. Pillows and cushions, like islands, littered the floor's blue carpet. In a far corner was the beast.

Jud walked towards it. The creature lay on its back, white arms clutching a pillow to its chest. Its long, pointed tongue hung from a corner of its mouth. Kneeling beside it, Jud pushed its snout with the gun barrel.

Dead.

Its lower body was sheathed with blood. He quickly checked, and saw that Lilly Thorn's description of the sex organ had been accurate. Amazed and disgusted, he backed away.

He climbed the wooden stairs and entered the kitchen of the windowless house.

## 2.

Axel Kutch, hunched like a wrestler in front of the attic door, grinned at Donna. His bald head gleamed in the light of her flare. Curly hair matted his bulky shoulders, his arms and chest and belly – but his penis stood hairless, thick and shiny and tilted high. He limped towards her.

'Stay back.'

He shook his head.

Threatening him with the flare, Donna tried to unsling her rifle.

A two-fingered hand grasped her wrist. It twisted sharply. The flare dropped, but he didn't stop twisting. Donna spun sideways, off balance, and fell to her back. Still clutching her wrist, Axel kicked her in the side. He

242

dropped to his knees. Picking up the flare, he jammed its unlighted end into a crack between the sofa cushions above Donna's head. Then he threw a leg over her. He sat on her belly, pinning her arms to the floor.

'You're beautiful,' he said.

She struggled, trying to free her arms.

'Stay still,' he said.

'Get off!'

'Stay still!'

Bending, he pushed his mouth against hers. She bit his lip, tasting the salty warmth of his blood, but he didn't stop kissing her. She bit again, savagely tearing the flesh of his lip. With a grunt, he pulled away. The back of his hand clubbed her face.

Weak from the blow, she tried with her free arm to shove him away.

He knocked her arm down, then punched her twice in the face.

Each blow was a stunning explosion of pain. Barely holding on to consciousness, she knew that he was tearing open her blouse. She heard buttons skitter across the floor, then felt the rough touch of his hands. Though her arms were free, she couldn't find strength to lift them. He pulled at her bra. When it wouldn't come off, he broke the shoulder straps. Donna felt the looseness, then the chilly bareness of her breasts. Axel squeezed them. The pain helped clear her mind. She felt the suck of his mouth. Then he was tugging at the belt of her corduroys.

She realized she could lift her arms. Opening her eyes, she saw Axel kneeling between her legs, head down as he worked to open her pants.

She reached behind her head. Stretched her arm. Grabbed the shaft of the flare. In a single swift motion, she plunged its sputtering head into Axel's eye. He shrieked as the room went dark. She shoved the flare harder. A warm wetness spilled on to her hand as the flare slid deep. Axel's rigid body bucked with convulsions. She pushed him off and rolled away from his body.

## 3.

Ahead of Jud, blue light glowed from the living room. He approached silently. He peered around the corner. The sight staggered him. Glancing to his left, he saw the front door. It was no more than six feet away.

Maggie and the creatures were probably thirty feet from him. One underneath her, would be slow getting free. The beast at her rear wouldn't be able to see him. But the one at her head was facing his way. He couldn't possibly make the door without it noticing him.

He pressed himself to the wall, out of sight. For several seconds, he listened to the grunting and the slippery smacking sounds. Maggie was gasping. From the violence of the sounds, he guessed that they would soon be done.

Once they were finished, his chance of escape . . .

Escape?

Christ, he'd almost forgotten what he'd come here to do.

He'd come here to kill the beast.

He'd come to stop it from murdering again.

Except it's not one beast, it's five. Maybe more. That doesn't change the purpose of the mission. It doesn't change the need for them to die. If anything, it increased the urgency of the task.

Lunging away from the wall, Judgement Rucker crouched and fired. A beast shrieked as the bullet crashed through its head. It stumbled backward, penis sliding from Maggie's mouth, ejaculating on to her face and hair.

The one behind her looked. Caught a bullet in its right eye. Slumped on to Maggie's back.

Jud held fire, watching Maggie struggle. The dead beast on her back fell away. She rolled off the live one, and lay on her side so that her body protected it from a shot by Jud.

Slowly, she stood up, being careful to shield the beast with her body. It got to its feet behind her. She began walking towards Jud.

'Bastard,' she muttered. 'Who do you think you are, bastard? Sneaking in here? Shooting us up? Killing my darlings?'

She kept limping towards him, dragging a leg that looked as if it had been chewed many years ago, and healed badly. Her ancient, swaying breasts were lined with scars and recent cuts, some bleeding. Blood dropped from her scarred shoulders and her neck. Jud knew why she wore a scarf in public.

'Stop,' he said.

'Bastard!'

'Damn it, I'll drop you!'

'No you won't.'

Suddenly, he heard snarling on the stairway behind him. He pivoted and fired at the darting shape. It shrieked but didn't stop. The claws of the beast with Maggie slashed across Jud's back. He lurched forward, turning, jerking the machete out of his belt. The claws swiped again. This time, he lopped off the creature's arm. He shot it once in the chest, then turned his gun to the beast leaping from beside the bannister post. His snapping finger blasted three holes into it. It fell.

Maggie dropped to her knees beside it. She hugged the white body, crooning, 'Oh Xanadu, Xanadu. Oh Xanadu!'

Her back was a disfigured mass of scar tissue and bleeding cuts.

'Oh Xanadu,' she sobbed, cradling the dead beast's head.

'Are there more?' Jud asked.

Maggie didn't answer. She didn't seem to hear.

Stepping around her and the body of Xanadu, Jud approached the stairway. He saw dim blue light in the upstairs hallway. Silently, he began to climb.

## 4.

Donna staggered down the front porch stairs. She slumped against the newel post, hugging it to keep from falling. The rifle strap slipped off her shoulder. She heard the walnut stock batter the railing. Probably put a scratch on the stock.

She wondered, vaguely, if the scratch would anger Jud. Men could be funny about that kind of thing.

God, would she ever see Jud again?

Where could he . . .?

A distant popping noise interrupted her question, and answered it. She raised her head. She heard more of the strange, low popping sounds, and she knew it was gunfire.

Gunfire muffled by the brick walls of the house without windows.

Watching the house, she heard another shot. Then three quick ones.

She started to run. The hanging rifle slapped her leg. Without slowing, she gripped the sling and swung the rifle in front of her. She gripped it solidly with both hands.

She glanced at the Chrysler, far to the right. Sandy's head was visible. The girl was locked in, safe.

Donna climbed awkwardly over the turnstile. She sprinted across the road. Then up the dirt driveway. She tried to remember if the rifle was cocked. Couldn't remember. As she ran, she worked the bolt. The ejected cartridge spun up and hit her face, its point jabbing her upper lip. Blinking tears away, she rammed another cartridge into the chamber.

Approaching the front of the dark house, she slowed

to a trot. She shifted the rifle to her left hand. Heavy. She propped its butt against her hip and pulled open the screen door. She tried the knob. Locked. The screen door swung back, bumping her shoulder.

Damn!

She aimed at the door crack next to the knob.

It's getting to be a habit, she thought.

The thought didn't amuse her,

## 5.

Cautiously, Jud stepped into the main bedroom. The mirrors exposed every corner. No beast. He looked inside the open closet. Satisfied that nothing would jump out at him, he stepped closer to the bed.

Wick Hapson, naked except for a leather vest, lay face down on the sheet. Chains anchored his wide-spread arms and legs to the bedposts. His face was turned to the left.

Kneeling, Jud looked into his eyes. They were wide with fear. His lips were trembling. 'Don't kill me,' he said. 'Christ it ain't my fault. I just gone along. I just *gone along!*'

As Jud left the room, he heard the blast of a gunshot downstairs.

## 6.

Donna drew back the bolt. As the shell spun out, she saw that the ammunition clip was empty. Her mind flashed a memory of the live cartridge stabbing her face and falling to the dirt driveway. No chance of finding it.

Okay, nobody had to know the rifle was empty.

She shouldered open the door and lurched back at the sight of two hideous beasts lying sprawled near the foot

247

of the stairway. Their shiny flesh looked pale blue. The severed arm of one lay near the wall.

Stepping around them, she glanced into the living room. Two more.

'Jud?' she called.

'Donna? Get out of here!'

His voice came from upstairs.

## 7.

Damn it! his mind screamed. What was Donna doing here?

He ran towards the last room, the room where he and Larry had heard strange breathing sounds that afternoon. The door was open slightly. Through the gap, he saw a blue light. He kicked the door, lunged into the room, and aimed at a pale figure crouched in a corner.

He held fire.

In the dim light, he saw dark hair hanging to her shoulders. She cradled something in her arms. An infant. It's snout, clamped on her dug, was sucking loudly.

Groaning, Jud backed towards the doorway.

## 8.

Donna, reaching the top of the stairs, saw the naked, ravaged form of Maggie Kutch limping towards the far end of the hall.

'Mom!'

Her head snapped to the side. Sandy, in tears, stood in the foyer looking up at her.

Donna looked again down the corridor. Maggie glanced back. Donna saw a butcher knife in the old woman's right hand. Donna shouldered the empty rifle. 'Drop it!' she shouted.

248

# 9.

Jud turned, faced Maggie, and started to raise his pistol. The knife plunged.

He was astonished.

He couldn't believe it.

That shiny, wide blade was actually vanishing into his chest.

She can't do this, he thought.

He tried to pull the trigger.

His hand didn't work.

*She can't!*

# Chapter Twenty-six

In the cold darkness of the crawlspace beneath the last cabin, Joni lay on her side. She hugged her knees close to her chest. She kept her teeth clenched tight to keep them from chattering.

The man would never find her here.

Never.

A long time ago, when she first got away, he hadn't even looked under the cabin. Maybe he would come back, though.

She didn't dare to move.

The dirt rocks dug into her skin, but she didn't move. Sometimes, itchy bugs crawled on her. She made believe they were caterpillars and lady bugs, and let them crawl.

The cold was worse than anything. It made her shake. If she shook too much, maybe the man would hear her, and catch her again.

A long time went by.

Then she heard something move nearby. An animal.

She held her breath.

Then she heard a quiet, 'Meeeow.'

The cat came up against her legs in the darkness, furry and warm and purring like a motor.

'Kitty,' she whispered.

She stroked its head and back.

The cat let her hold it. She held it lightly against her chest. Its purr was so loud she worried the man would hear it and find her.

Soon she was no longer shaking.

A sound from above startled the cat. It leapt away and disappeared.

Joni listened closely.

Footsteps on the cabin floor.

She heard the door swing open. She saw bare feet on the stairs at the front of the cabin.

'Girl?' she called.

The legs stopped at the bottom of the stairs.

'Girl?'

The legs turned. The girl crouched and looked through the darkness of the crawlspace. 'You under there?' she asked.

'Yeah.'

'You gonna stay there all night?'

'Is he gone?'

'Yeah, I think so. It's been hours. Took me that long to get untied.'

Getting to her hands and knees, Joni began to crawl through the darkness towards her waiting friend.

# *Epilogue*

'When will they take the chains off?'

'When they figure we won't run away,' Donna said.

'I wouldn't run away.'

Donna, squinting through dark, could see only a white blur where her daughter sat among the pillows. 'I would. I'd run away in a second.'

'Why?'

'We're prisoners.'

'Don't you like it?' Sandy asked.

'No.'

'Don't you like Rosy?'

'No.'

'I do. Except she's ugly like Axel.'

'They're twins, she ought to be.'

'She's a retard.'

'Yeah.'

'Who do you like better, Seth or Jason?'

'Neither.'

'I like Seth better,' Sandy said.

'Oh.'

'Aren't you gonna ask me why?'

'No.'

'Come on, Mom. Just 'cause you're mad they killed Jud. Besides, they didn't even kill him, Maggie did. And he deserved it, too.'

'Sandy!'

'Look how many of them he murdered. Six! God, he deserved it. He deserved a lot worse.'

'Damn it, shut up!' And then she was ashamed for using such language on her daughter.

'At least he didn't get Seth and Jason,' Sandy said.

'Too bad he didn't.'

'You're just saying that. You're just saying that to spoil things. You like them I know you do. I'm not deaf, you know.'

'Well, I don't like being chained up in the dark. I don't like that at all. And the food stinks.'

'Maggie might let you start cooking, if you ask her. Wick told me I can drive with him to Santa Rosa, one of these days, and pick up groceries. Once they trust us more, we can do all kinds of stuff.'

'I'd sure like to see the sun again.'

'Me too. Mom?'

'Yes?'

'Do you still think you're pregnant?'

'I think so.'

'Who's baby do you think it is? Jason, I bet.'

'I don't know.

'I'd like to have Seth's baby.'

'Shhh. I think they're coming.'